THE TWO TENLEYS

Elsa Kurt

ELSA KURT

<u>DEDICATION</u>

For my husband, always.

ELSA KURT

<u>CONTENTS</u>

[1] TENLEY NUMBER ONE

Compensating for something, much?

That was Ten's first though at seeing the silver-haired doctor behind his massive mahogany desk. She'd smirked then, but not now. Now Tenley Harper blinked at him, failing to comprehend the words he'd spoken when she sat down. He tried again, this time enunciating each word.

"I am very sorry, Mrs. Harper, but there is nothing we can do. This type of tumor—it's called a *glioblastoma*. It's an... inoperable brain tumor. Based on the size, you have—at best—six to ten months."

Ten blinked harder at the doctor. "But—but I just came in for my—how is this…"

Dr. Rue looked ruefully at her. *How à propos. Dr. Rue feels rueful.* She stifled an entirely inappropriate laugh. *Ah, this is what hysteria feels like. I am… hysterical. Isn't that hysterical?*

The doctor cleared his throat, glanced at the expensive watch on his wrist and said, "Mrs. Harper, the tumor affects your cognitive abilities. Short-term memory loss, confusion, difficulty processing information. You must schedule a follow-up appointment with Dr. Kerns for… planning."

Ten didn't move. She couldn't. Her ass had glued itself to the leather seat, her legs were rubber, and her feet cement. Dr. Rue straightened, replaced the *compassionate doctor giving bad news* face with an *I have many other patients to see* expression.

He coughed, averted his gaze, and said, "I can only tell you what the chart says. We can give you the names of some other doctors if you'd like a second opinion, but Dr. Kerns is considered one of the best in the state. If he's diagnosed a brain tumor, it's a brain tumor. You… you really should have someone accompanying you on these appointments from now on, Mrs. Harper."

"Miss."

Now Dr. Rue blinked. "Pardon?"

"It's *Miss* Harper," said Ten.

Because that's a super important clarification to make right now. Wait, it is. The guy's giving you a death sentence; at least he can get your name right.

Dr. Rue awarded her with a polite—if not patronizing—smile. "Very well. *Miss* Harper. Do you have someone to drive you home?"

"No, I—"

"Again, you really should lean on the help of your loved ones at this time. There are many effects of a brain tumor. Seizures, for one. You wouldn't want that to happen while you were driving, now would you?"

He shook his head, coaxing her to do the same. As if Ten were a daft child in need of coaching. Vaguely insulted, very baffled, and totally shocked, Ten shook her head. Just like an obedient, daft child.

Dr. Rue offered a small, closed lip smile and stood. Tenley stood as well. Somehow, her rubber legs supported her. He tilted his head toward the office door.

Ten reached for her purse and said, "T-thank you, Dr. Rue," and left the office.

Thank you? Why did I say thank you? Thank you for giving me the worst news of my life, then sending me home without so much as a lollipop. A lollipop? Why would I expect a lollipop? This isn't the pediatrician, for God's sake. It must be the tumor. Oh, my fucking God. I have a tumor.

Ten walked through the reception area on legs that felt disconnected from her body. Like someone had attached them onto her torso and moved them by remote control. Left foot—lift, step—right foot—lift, step. Repeat. She imagined her arms extended out like planks, realized that was more of a zombie walk, and corrected the mental image to arms bent at the elbows, chop, chop chopping the air.

What the fuck is wrong with me? Why am I thinking about zombies and robots? Oh, because I have a fucking tumor. That's why.

On her arrival at the office, there'd been three other people. One had been a crabby old lady who'd knitted with the kind of aggression usually reserved for a stabbing. The *tick, tick, tick* of her needles, loud in the otherwise quiet office, made Ten a little stabby, too. She and her aggressive needles were gone.

Still waiting was leathery-skinned, middle-aged man in absurdly colored plaid pants that screamed, *I'm retired! I play golf every day! I love the early bird special and Bloody Mary's in the morning!* He looked up from a dog-eared *People* magazine—Jennifer Lopez graced the cover—and frowned at her.

The third, a cute guy in a motorcycle jacket and huge black boots, was nowhere in sight. Ten had spent her own waiting time thinking carnal thoughts about motorcycle jacket guy. Could it have only been fifteen minutes ago that she'd been thinking dirty thoughts about a stranger in a waiting room? Now, she was dying. It was a bizarre leap of circumstances. Correction. She'd apparently been dying then, too, but just hadn't known it. Ten wanted to be the Ten of fifteen minutes ago. *Blissful ignorance come back, you bitch.*

In the meantime, several more seats had been taken up. The television bolted in the far corner had been turned on. On it, a show Ten couldn't stand. The one with the three screechy women who argued all the time with the fourth one. What was the point of it all? Ten abhorred daytime television. Although, in less than ten months, Ten's option to abhor or love anything will have run out. Forever.

She staggered, then sat down hard in the nearest seat. A petite, sunglasses-wearing blonde sat one chair over. The woman jumped away, pressing herself to the arm of her seat. Once she saw Ten's shell-shocked, pallid face, she softened.

"Are you—are you all right?"

Ten was not all right. In fact, Ten might pass out. The woman beside her thought so, too.

"Listen," she said, lifting her glasses onto the top of her head, "breathe in through your nose—one, two, three, four—and out through your mouth. Good. Again."

After about three times of this, Ten released a shaky breath and said, "Thank you. I, uh, just got some unexpected news, and I—"

"Say no more. I'm expecting unwanted news myself. I already know what they'll say, but—"

"Gotta keep the faith, right?"

The woman's smile was mournful. "Yeah, sure."

Ten guessed her to be about her own age—thirty-six—but she could've been younger... or older. The delicate blonde woman had a pretty face, but pinched, like everything offended or pained her. That look gave way to one of weary resignation, like she was someone used to bad news.

For a moment, Ten had the notion she should try to comfort *her*. Then her phone rang. She'd forgotten to silence it, so *It Takes Two* by Rob Base blared across the small waiting area. It had seemed a hilarious idea to download the ringtone after a drunken night of karaoke. Now, not so much. Her waiting room mates jumped and scowled at her.

Ten sprang up, called out an apology, and hurried outside. She forgot the petite blonde before the door clicked shut.

Breathless, she spoke into the receiver. "Hello?"

Margot yelled, "Jesus, when are you getting here?"

In the background, Carlos and Lucy piped in, "We're wait-*ing*."

"Shit. Fuck. I forgot. I'll be there in fifteen."

Ten threw the phone back in her purse and fished out her keys. Weekly brunch at Cappy's with her three besties. It was their *thing*. How could she have forgotten? *The brain tumor, duh*. It would explain so much.

Her phone rang again. Josh. Double shit. She debated, her finger hovering over 'ignore.' Maybe she *should* answer his call. Tell him, *Josh, I have news. I have an inoperable brain tumor. I can't put you through this, I care too much about you. Go, live your life. Find love. Never forget me.*

Jesus, was she really considering using her brain tumor as some morbid break up line? Yes, yes, she was. But what if he dug his heels in and said he wanted to be there for her? Ugh. That would suck. He was a sweet guy, great body. Fun to be—what the hell was she thinking? How could she be thinking such pedestrian thoughts at such a time?

Shock, you twit. That explained it. Her thoughts were way too... too *Ten* for someone who just got diagnosed with a terminal illness. She must be in shock. Ten blinked at the dashboard of her convertible Volkswagen bug, waiting and expecting to cry. Nothing happened. *Okay.* The reality would hit her soon enough. It had to. But right then—with the Florida sun shining down on her scalp and the fragrance of the Jacarandas drifting on the salty sea air—she felt fine.

"Might as well enjoy it while it lasts." *Denial... it ain't just a river in Egypt. Ba-dum-bump.*

Ten reached around to the back seat and felt for her bright red, wide-brimmed hat. She plunked it on her head, twisted her hair into a loose braid and flipped down the visor. The rectangle mirror showed the same face she'd been seeing her whole life. Green eyes. Suntanned face. Freckled nose—a bit longer than she'd like—and a full mouth. She looked... healthy.

"There's nothing wrong with you, Harper. You're fine."

You're fine repeated in her head and didn't stop until her tires crunched over the sandy parking lot of Cappy's on the Beach.

<u>²TENLEY NUMBER TWO</u>

By the time Tenley 'Lee' Harper's watch read eleven-eleven, the frazzled nurse had pushing seven people through check-in, pre-exam, exam, and check out, before finally walking her into the office of Keaton Rue. Lee was the last patient, according to the nurse, and by the way the woman kept looking at the clock above the door, she wanted to get this appointment over and done with. Lee opened her mouth to express her offense at being rushed, but the dark-haired woman spoke first.

"Eleven-eleven," said Maria. "Make a wish."

Lee blinked and said, "Make a—a wish?"

"Yeah, you know. It's like, lucky or something." She looked down at Lee's chart, then back up again. "Oh, so you're our second—"

From somewhere down the hall, a man's voice called, "Maria? Have you seen my glasses?"

The woman slumped and gave Lee an, *ugh, men,* look—which Lee disapproved of. This was her place of employment, after all and that was unprofessional. Nurse Maria left Lee alone in the office. Whatever she'd been about to say obviously hadn't been important.

Once the nurse had gone, she sat in one of the two chairs facing an especially large—distastefully large—desk and closed her eyes. "I wish the doctor will have good news for me." She repeated it three times, then opened her eyes to see Dr. Rue staring at her.

"Miss Harper, I'm happy to say your results look normal. You are in overall excellent health, blood pressure fine, cholesterol, perfect. Bloodwork shows iron deficiency, though. Get some iron supplements. Take two a day the first week, then one a day. If there are no questions—"

"Did you say… normal? But—"

"Now, now, Miss Harper, no need to look for a problem where there's none, right?"

"Mrs."

"Pardon?"

"It's *Mrs.* Harper, not Miss."

Dr. Rue frowned a moment as if he were trying to recall something. Lee watched as his eye caught the clock on the far wall, just like his nurse's had. She looked, too. Eleven sixteen. He clapped his hands together, startling her, and declared, "You're as healthy as a horse, Miss—Mrs. Harper. No need to schedule a follow up unless your symptoms don't improve." He stood and shuttled her to the door. "Have a lovely afternoon."

Tenley 'Lee' Harper allowed him to herd her out the door, her face a riot of tremulous smiles, quivering chin, and rapidly blinking eyes. "I—I— thank you, Dr. Rue. You don't know what this means to me. You—you can't imagine. Dr. Kerns had made it sound so—"

"You're quite welcome, my dear. I'll give Dr. Kerns your regards."

He held the door open wide and all but pushed her out at eleven-nineteen. *Goodness, was* he *ever in a hurry. Terrible doctor-patient skills*. She'd have to write a letter of complaint. Were doctor's offices on Yelp? Surely, they must... and it hit her.

I don't have a brain tumor. I'm... not... dying.

Lee Harper, behind the wheel of her silver Prius, reached a shaking hand for her phone.

"Kenny? Yes, I've just left the doctor's office. No, actually. Quite the opposite." What Tenley said next surprised even her. "I—I want a divorce, Kenny."

She hit the 'end' key on his—likely stunned— silence, pulled down the visor and gazed at her reflection in the small mirror, and smiled. Lee Harper just got a new lease on life. *And I'm not wasting a single second of it.*

<u>³ DR.RUE & NURSE MARIA</u>

Early that morning...

"Dr. Rue?"

"Yes, Maria?"

"I've just heard from Dr. Kerns. He won't be making it in today, I'm afraid. Bad case of the flu, it seems. He has four patients in the waiting room. Can you cover them? There's eight patients counting yours."

Dr. Rue sighed, irritated. *This* is why he'd resisted group practice until now. He'd scheduled a round of golf at noon. He glanced at the clock. Nine-fifteen. He supposed he could squeeze them in. Keaton Rue calculated. If he allotted one minute for chart review, gave them only nine minutes each, allowing for five minutes of pre-exam work up for the nurses... yes, he could make a noon tee off.

"Well. Let's get started."

Nurse Rodriguez sifted through the charts, frowned, then laughed in surprise. "Wow, you and Dr. Kerns have patients with the same name. I've never even heard this one before, and now there's two in one day. Yours is a new patient, and his is coming in for some bad news. Make sure you—"

Dr. Rue had already walked away. Maria Rodriguez shook her head. *Typical.* She just needed to get through the day, then off to ten days in Aruba for her and Luis. No work, no worries.

The doctor pushed each patient through quickly, much more so than Dr. Kerns ever did. Concern over the speed at which they worked tempted Maria to say something, but the image of the open suitcase on her bed made her bite her tongue.

At eleven-eleven—after pushing seven people through check-in, pre-exam, exam, and check out on her own—the frazzled nurse walked the last patient, the second Tenley Harper, into the office of Keaton Rue.

"Eleven-even," said Maria. "Make a wish."

The petite blonde blinked and said, "Make a—a wish?"

"Yeah, you know. It's like, lucky or something."

In record time, Dr. Rue received and consulted the patient and then held the door open wide and all but pushed her out at eleven-nineteen. He would be in his Lexus by eleven-thirty, on the highway by eleven-thirty-five. Exactly as planned. Maria Rodriguez would be on her merry way as well once she flicked off the lights and locked the doors. By noon, the office was dark and empty and the last three—doctor, nurse, and patient—left with smiles and relief.

⁴ <u>JOSH</u>

The dull ring of Tenley's cell phone rang in Josh Duffy's ear until it went to the 'mailbox is full message.' He hit end and tossed it back into his gym bag. He pictured her sitting in her car, or maybe walking along the street with that giant dog of hers. Or maybe sitting on the beach pretending to be a painter. She's no painter, for Christ's sake. No more than she was a dog sitter, or a life coach, or a hypnotherapist, or any of the other things she printed off online certification awards for.

In his mind's eye, he saw her pause, glance down at the phone in her hand, shrug and put it away again. A move so... so *Ten*. She never cared about other people's feelings, least of all Josh's. Ten Harper was a *narcissist*. At least that's what Kline was saying in between curls.

"*Classic* narcissist, to be exact." He dropped his weights on the mat and added, "But she's a stone-cold fox, so who cares, man? Just get it in, bro. Tap that ass, homie. Give her the—"

Josh also dropped his dumbbell down onto the mat with a thud and clank. "I get it, man. Shut up. She's not—it's not like that," said Josh, punching Kline hard in the arm.

Kline didn't understand. Josh had fallen in love with Ten. He didn't mean for it to happen, but it did. One minute it was just sex, the next... boom. He couldn't stop *thinking* about her. Not just sexual thoughts, either. In the beginning, sure. He'd be taking a shower, picture her ass or her perky tits, and hello—his rock-hard soldier standing at attention. It's not even that they had crazy or kinky sex. The only word for it was—he'd never say the word out loud—*sensual*. Ten fucked as if they were the only thing that existed in the entire world.

"Aw, shit, man," said Kline in between bench presses, "don't tell me you're falling for her. Dude, that's the kiss of death with a chick like that."

"A chick like *what*," asked Josh, his fist ready for another shot.

Kline sighed and sat up. He lifted the hem of his shirt, revealing a sun-browned six-pack, and wiped his face on it. "Psssh, an older, rich chick. That's what. You're a boy toy. Face it. Shit, *enjoy* it."

They moved on to legs. In between presses, Josh exhaled and said, "She's not old, asshole."

Ten didn't work, not like regular people worked. She drove a butter-cream-yellow convertible Volkswagen Bug, shared a long, one level Spanish villa-style house with her former pro-wrestler dad—the fake wrestling, all scripted like a soap opera on steroids—her giant dog, Fitz and her little dog, Lizzy.

The crème-white and burnt-sienna trimmed home had arched entrances half covered by climbing ivy and clematis, a row of Jacaranda trees standing sentry, and a gated, cobblestone curved driveway. An expansive gourmet kitchen opened to a pool with elaborate landscaping and a small guesthouse.

Josh had firsthand knowledge that Ten's bedroom had French doors that opened to a gorgeous view of the ocean. She'd designed an oasis in the smallish part of backyard—a koi pond she dug herself, a vegetable garden, and flowers everywhere. He loved hanging out there almost as much as he loved having sex with her.

Kline interrupted his thoughts. "Face it, bro. She's you're sugar mama. You're twenty-six, she's thirty-six. You go out to dinner, what, like three nights a week—on her dime."

Seeing Josh's face, he exclaimed, "What, am I wrong? Anyhow, she never works, and she's always buying you shit. If that ain't sugar mama game, bro..." Kline let the sentence drop and shrugged. Then, "Trust me man, you ain't in love. You in *lust*."

Kline stood and thrust his hips back and forth a few times in what he probably thought a provocative way. It got him several dirty looks from the women nearby and eliminate any chance of bagging a single one.

"See, *this* is why you get zero play. You have no game, man. And stop doing that. People are going think we're gay."

That served as all the encouragement Kline needed to turn on his full, 'I'm a total dick' act. He tried to hump Josh's leg, bellowing, "I don't care who knows about our love, Joshie baby."

A blonde—built like a gymnast—rolled her eyes, snatched up her water bottle and strode away.

Not before giving Josh a once over and a smile though. Kline noticed it, too.

"You see that, man? Even when they think you're *gay*, they still want a piece of you. You're *twenty-six*. You're in your prime, dude. I'm tellin' you, get one of these ripe specimens here, take her back to your place, rock her world. You'll get your power back, bro. Guaranteed."

Josh did not take Kline's advice. He went home, checked his phone for messages, showered and got dressed. He checked his phone again, then checked in on his virtual clients via email. Three were training for body-building competitions, two just wanted to lose weight, one he suspected of just trying to hook up, and a new client. He suspected she would drop out of the program before she'd made it through a month.

People always think they want a personal trainer to tell them what to eat... until a personal trainer tells them what to do and what to eat. Or, more accurately, what *not* to do or eat. So far this Lee chick had asked for a dozen modifications or switches to her meal plans and complained about the suggested workout schedule. Four on, three off.

Not too much to ask for, but apparently, she disagreed. He checked his phone again.

⁵ LEE

Lee waited, slunk low behind her steering wheel with her sunglasses on; like a cop on a stakeout about to get made. Or so she imagined. She didn't watch those kinds of shows or read those kinds of books. They triggered her anxiety. At any second, Kenny's blue Prius would back out of the driveway and go left, toward the middle school. Of *course*, he still came home for lunch. Predictable even in crisis. Unless Kenny *wasn't* in crisis. Maybe he, too, had wanted a divorce all along, and had just been waiting for her to be the one to say it first. She could see him doing something like that. It's what *she'd* been doing, after all.

The moment the brake lights went off, and his Prius turned left, Lee sat up straight, put the car in drive and her hands instinctively at three and nine on the wheel, then promptly dropped one hand into her lap.

No more following every rule. You're a-a rebel now.

Her eyes darted around as if Kenny might jump out in front of her. She caught her gaze in the rearview mirror.

"Stop being silly, Lee."

Lee giggled. Since leaving the doctor's office her moods swung from euphoria to fear and back again. Had she really told her husband of nearly fifteen years she wanted a divorce? She giggled again.

"Lee Harper, this is no laughing matter. And stop talking to yourself."

This, she found funny as well. Picturing Kenny's sad face sobered her. A little. Not nearly as much as it should have. Kenny was a good man. A good husband, too. Everything about Kenny Harper radiated *good*. Maybe that was the problem.

Lee and Kenny met in college, both going for their bachelor's degree, both planning to become teachers. Their goals aligned, their temperaments complimented, and their courtship rolled along into their engagement, which culminated to their wedding and marriage. The only thing that didn't go according to plan? Children.

The Harpers tried for eight years to bring a baby into the world, but the universe had other ideas. This is what Kenny would say when someone—too many someone's, in Lee's opinion—asked them when they would have kids. Lee said nothing, she couldn't.

They tried adopting, but were twice led to the brink of joy, only to suffer disappointment so crushing, Lee couldn't get out of bed for a week. Shades drawn. Lights off. Just her and the deafening silence of a house with no children.

They fostered for a few years, but the goodbyes were too wretched for either to bear. So, they adopted Dexter, a three-year-old, blue-eyed Himalayan cat with a crooked tail and a bad temper.

Lee pulled into the narrow driveway of 123 Bluebird Lane, pressing the button for the garage door as she did. Their neighbor, Eddie, waved from the forsythia hedges dividing the two yards. Lee sighed, waving back. He'd insist on talking to her about the upcoming association meeting. Kenny and Eddie were on the board and took their volunteer jobs way too seriously, even for Lee's stickler-for-rules taste. She approved enforcement of guidelines, but they didn't need to talk it to death every darn day.

Death. That monster she'd been so sure coming for her, now seemed a vague and distant a concept. Life gave her more time on the clock, and Lee had no intention of wasting another minute of. As soon as she got inside, she would open her laptop pick a destination, and book a trip. For one. Where should she go? Somewhere warm. Somewhere—

"Hey ya, neighbor," called Eddie.

Lee closed the car door and gritted her teeth. "Hey, Eddie. How's it going?"

"Oh, you know. Retirement, loving every minute. Have you ever seen our yard look more beautiful? Betcha haven't. See you and Kenny at the meeting tonight, right? Joan and Bill are hosting. We're gonna vote on the Levin's pool request. If you ask me, Lee, we should all—"

"Sorry, Eddie, but I've got to get inside to—"

"Sure, sure. No worries. Oh, did Kenny tell you about the big to-do over the gazebo? Seems the Collin's want to paint it blue. Blue, can you imagine? You can't make it *blue*, I said to Vic. Well, Carol just had a fit over that. She said—"

"Eddie," said Lee.

"I—yes?"

"I don't give a-a *fuck* about the gazebo. Paint it hot pink for all I care. Oh, and tell Carol Collins to go fuck herself, okay? Great. See you later, Eddie."

Lee left a slack-jawed Eddie Catania staring after her long after she'd closed the front door. Her cheeks flamed and her heart raced. Had she just said the F-word? *Twice*?

"Oh, my."

Setting her purse on the foyer table, she checked her reflection in the ornate mirror above the table. Still the same Lee staring back at her. Or was it? She squinted and chicken-bobbed her head forward, then tilted her head this way and that. People still thought she was in her twenties. Well, one person. Last week, the young man at the package store took her ID and said, "Damn, girl, I thought you were, like, twenty-five, twenty-six. You a MILF."

She didn't know what 'milf' meant until she'd looked it up at home. Then she was glad she hadn't asked Kenny if he'd heard the term. She doubted it, anyhow. Kenny watched the History Channel and Food Network. He read books about Lincoln, the Civil War, Ulysses Grant.

Neither he nor Lee fell under their young student's idea of *cool teachers*. Not like the Phys Ed. Teacher, Chuck D'Ambrosio—Mr. D. as the kids called him—who referred to them as *dude* or *homie* and high-fived them when they walked into the gym. Not like Miss. Palmieri, who wore rock concert t-shirts on casual Fridays and had a strip of peacock-blue hair, and—she didn't tell Kenny about this part—had her belly button pierced. Her belly button!

Lee could've gone along in her existence without knowing this information about their new reading specialist, but the girl had taken a shine to Lee and confided in her the day after she got the piercing.

"Hey, Tenley, guess what I did last night?"

"It's Lee. Just Lee."

Miss. Palmieri—Rachel—blinked at her.

"It's just—well, only my brother called me Ten. He had developmental delays, so you know, I just—he—you were saying?"

"Right, so anyhow, you'll never guess who I went out with last night or what we did. Okay, technically, what I did. He dared me to."

Lee held her mug of tea high and close to her chest, her elbows jutting out. She gave Rachel a polite but tight smile and looked around the teacher's lounge for Kenny. Instead, she caught the eye of the math teacher, Rose Brackenworth, who looked Rachel up and down with an undisguised sneer. Rachel followed Lee's gaze, rolled her eyes and turned her back to Mrs. Brackenworth.

"Never mind that old bat. Look," said Rachel, lifting the hem of her blouse to reveal a silver stud poking out of the top of her belly button. "It's a little sore, but I love it. Don't you?"

"Oh, I—it's—wow. What did—"

"Now, guess who I went out with."

Rachel's eyes gleamed with giddy mischief and she'd yet to pull her shirt back down. Lee averted her eyes and flapped her hand in the general vicinity of the young teacher's midriff. When Rachel didn't take the hint, Lee whispered, "Rachel, people are looking."

Rachel laughed and said, "Oh, Lee, you are too gorgeous to be this uptight. Relax. And who cares what they think. Old goats. Now ask me who I went out with last night, will you?"

Lee sighed. "Chuck D'Ambrosio?"

"*Yes*. Oh, my God, how did you know?"

Because you two flirt every day and it's impossible not to notice. Lee instead said, "Lucky guess?"

Lee learned more about Chuck in the following fifteen minutes than she ever wanted to know. Suffice to say, she blushed every time she saw him afterwards. Something else about that conversation stuck in her mind. Rachel had called the other teachers—many of which were about the same age as Lee—old goats, but *her* gorgeous. No one had called her that before. Pretty, yes. Cute, many times.

Her high school boyfriend, Mark, called her hot once. Kenny, when they were dating, called her beautiful. But he'd been sloppy drunk—off two beers, nonetheless—so she found it hard to take seriously.

Gorgeous applied to women who shopped in Nordstrom and wore makeup, not ones who bought their clothes in the juniors or petites sections of JC Penny and who owned five pairs of sensible shoes, three pairs of practical boots, one pair of running sneakers, and one pair of tennis sneakers. It wasn't a term for women whose hairstyle hadn't changed in twenty years—blunt, shoulder-length bob, trimmed every six weeks. Gorgeous didn't apply to women who said phrases like *easy-peasy or* ate egg salad sandwiches on wheat for lunch.

Women like Lee Harper were the girl-next-door's younger sister—almost as pretty as their sibling, but not quite. The Lee's of the world dated the nice boys who tutored the jocks. Then they married those nice boys, got office jobs with decent salaries and good benefits, and had between one and four children in short order. They baked cookies for the bake sales and wore cardigans.

At least, that's how Lee envisioned her life before her body failed to produce offspring. She'd always thought they'd get a dog, too. For the kids, naturally. Children should grow up with pets, she believed. It would have been a small dog, though. Like a Shih Tzu or a Havanese. The Harpers weren't a Labrador or Retriever family. Those dogs were for the girl-next-door families.

"Bullshit."

Her voice in the quiet house startled her. Lee squinted at her reflection and repeated the swear. "Bull *shit.* I can have any kind of dog I want. I can pierce my belly button, too."

She didn't actually want to pierce her belly button though. She tapped her chin. "No, a tattoo. That's what I'll get."

Satisfied, she left the foyer and strode into the kitchen. A pang too strong to call mere hunger carved a notch in her belly. *Ravenous.* that's how Lee felt. In the refrigerator there were—among the usual contents—seven single serve yogurts, six pre-made kale and quinoa salads, a container or egg salad, another of tuna salad, and a whole, store-made rotisserie chicken which she'd planned make chicken salad from. Out of habit, she reached for the yogurt. A sensible, healthy, filling snack in between meals. Her hand hovered, then reached for the chicken.

At the counter by the sink, Lee tore off the plastic dome and cast it aside. She stared at the bird for a moment. Then, she ripped off a leg and devoured it, right down to the bone. She ate almost half the chicken this way, discarding bones into the sink and wiping the dripping grease from her mouth and chin with the back of her sleeve. Her hair stuck to her cheek and she brushed it back with her wrist.

Once her stomach was full, thirst overcame her. Behind the bottled water and cans of seltzer, there stood a six pack of an IPA someone had gifted Kenny some time ago. Lee took two cans and marched upstairs, peeling off her soiled top and dropping it on the floor as she went. At the top, she cracked open the first can, drank it all, and tossed it down the stairs. Splatters of beer studded the runner, walls, and banister as the can tumbled and clanked. Lee shrugged and strolled into the bedroom, now only in her bra and skirt.

On the top shelf of her side of the closet an old, powder-blue suitcase slept. She pulled it down and threw it on the bed. At her dresser she yanked open each drawer, grabbing handfuls of this and that—bras, underpants, socks, jeans, tops—and pitched them into the open mouth of the suitcase with no care of wrinkles or proper packing.

She did much the same back at her closet, sweeping an armload of light sweaters and dresses—hangers still on—and shoved them on top of the rest. Once she could fit no more, Lee closed and latched the suitcase. It took considerable effort, and articles of clothing stuck out of every edge, but it closed well enough to lug downstairs and out to the Prius.

Eddie still trolled around outside, watering his grass now.

"Oh, you going on a trip? Not before the meeting, I hope. Say, is that your…"

Eddie, staring at her bra, colored crimson. The forgotten hose now watered the driveway. Lee ignored him and went back inside. Her cell phone rang as she walked in. It would be Kenny, calling in between classes.

"Hello, Kenny," said Lee, sounding bored.

"Lee, listen. I understand. You've been under a lot of stress these few weeks. I know you don't mean it about the—" he whispered into the receiver, "*divorce*."

"*These few weeks*," she repeated back to him. "No, Kenny. *Years*. Years, and years, and years. Tell Connie I'm resigning, effective immediately. Goodbye, Kenny. And please don't call again. I'll— I'll call you when I'm ready."

She hung up, her hands shaking. Once again, she caught her reflection in the mirror and steeled herself. "You're not *her* anymore, Lee. Snap out of it."

An unexpected image popped into her head. The woman in the doctor's office who'd staggered and sat down beside her. Now, *she* exemplified gorgeousness. Lee had observed her drift across the waiting room in a trance. Her gaze unfocused, her gait uneven. Lee's first thought? *She's drunk*. Or on the drugs. She looked the type. A modern-day hippie, sun-kissed blonde hair to her waist, a gauzy floral print blouse with a red bra clearly visible underneath, her tan, flat midriff peeking out between the knot in the blouse and her harem-style pants. She wore strappy-sandals and turquoise and bead jewelry. Lee found that she envied the woman's free-spiritedness, if not the drug use.

But when she sat down, Lee saw her expression. It was shock. It didn't take a genius to put two and two together. The woman had received bad news. Just like Lee expected to. Her envy and disdain melted into sympathy. The nurturer in her took over and she guided the woman through a breathing exercise she'd always found helpful during her own, frequent times of anxiety.

Before Lee could ask her name, the woman's phone rang, and she jumped up to answer it. She ran out the door in a flash, leaving behind the scent of bergamot and rose in her wake. Then came Lee's turn to see the doctor, so thoughts of the hippie woman faded. Until now. Lee shook out her hair to make it look a little wilder, less salon perfect. She'd always worn it parted slightly off-center, but now she combed her fingers through and split it down the middle. The change could not be called drastic, but she *did* look different. Not quite carefree, but casual.

Upstairs again, Lee surveyed what remained in her closet. Wedged in the back corner, behind her winter coat, hung an outfit she'd bought for Halloween several years back, but never wore. She and Kenny were to go as Sonny and Cher to the school dance. At the last minute, Lee changed her mind. *Chickened out*, was more like it. Kenny still wore his outfit, which looked even more ridiculous on its own. Lee had dressed in her usual attire— dress pants, blouse, cardigan. She accessorized with a light-up Jack-O-Lantern necklace, but she didn't switch on the little light.

The Cher outfit that had once looked absurd and garish, now radiated sexiness and freedom. Faded denim bell-bottoms, orange crop top, camel-colored, fringe vest. Lee tore—not cut—the tags off and yanked the clothes on. At the full-length mirror in the bedroom's corner, she admired her new look.

"Something's not quite right," said Lee, biting her bottom lip. She grinned. Contorting her arms around her back, Lee unclasped her bra under the crop top and slid it off through one armhole. The boring beige undergarment dangled from between her thumb and forefinger. With disdain, she said, "Goodbye and good riddance, plain Jane," before flinging it across the room.

The feel of her bare breasts—modest B cups that had kept their perkiness—as they swayed against the soft cotton of her shirt exhilarated Lee. The old Lee would've folded her arms over her chest, hiding and immobilizing them. Not the new Lee. This version of herself loved the air on her skin, the friction of material against her nipples. She loved the cool wood floor beneath her bare feet as she padded down the stairs, and most of all, Lee loved her new lease on life.

A twinge of guilt flitted through her heart at the sight of Dexter sleeping on the windowsill. He'd barely lifted his head when she came in. Still, maybe she should take him?

"Dexter? You want to go for a ride? Huh, buddy? Dex?"

In response, Dexter stared at Lee through slitted eyes, then raised a paw to his face and groomed himself with the languid insolence all cats seem to inherently master from birth. He always did like Kenny better.

She exhaled a hard gust of air through her nose and said, "Have it your way, Dex. See ya around."

Ten minutes later, Lee drove barefoot along the highway, windows down and country music blaring as loud as the little car speakers would allow. Even the moonroof let in air and light, a first since she and Kenny bought the matching cars last year.

She asked her reflection, "Well, New Lee, where should we go?"

Her first dilemma since trading in her old life. *Think, Lee, think. Where would new you go?* She glanced at the fringe on her vest and the hippie woman's face flashed in her mind. *Where would* she *go?* As that though floated around, a looming billboard caught Lee's eye.

Forget Your Cares at Cappy's On The Beach!
Colds Drinks and Live Music Daily!
Next Exit

The beach. That's where someone like the hippie woman would go.

"No, that's where someone like New Lee would go," corrected Lee with a Cheshire grin.

[6] TEN

Meanwhile, at that exact beach restaurant, Ten knocked back her third drink. Margot, Lucy, and Carlos forgave her forgetfulness when she ordered and paid for their second round.

"So, you never said how your doctor's appointment went," said Margot.

Ten waited a beat. The trio stared at her. Margot slurped the remains of her margarita through her paper straw, Carlos fanned himself, and Lucy tried to catch the eye of their waitress.

"Right as rain," said Ten. "Picture of health," she added.

"Cheers, big ears," said Carlos.

"I'd raise my glass but it's empty," said Margot.

Lucy said, "Thank God. All you ever hear these days is bad news. I'm *tired* of bad news. I knew you'd be fine, though. I sent you healing energy thoughts with my distance Reiki. Did you feel it?"

"I think—"

"Can we get another round?" Lucy caught the waitress and promptly forgot about her healing Reiki powers.

"No more for me," said Ten, "I've got to get home to Fitz and Lizzy. Dad's been with them all day."

"Aw, party pooper," pouted Margot. "Well, give those two fabulous poochies some smoochies from Auntie Go-Go."

Ten laughed, "I will. And leave the Vespa here if you're too loopy to drive. Understood?" To Carlos, she said, "And you, good luck on your date tonight. What's his name again?"

"Hector," said Carlos, rolling the 'r' and fluttering his lashes.

"Right. Do everything I would do and more, you heathen. Lu-Lu, yoga tomorrow?"

"You got it, sista. Hey, you sure you're all good? You look a little... I don't know, off."

"What?" Ten's voice had gone an octave too high. She coughed and tried to laugh her off, "Puh-lease, I'm better than good. I'm super-fly, mamma."

Margot raised her new margarita and said, "Hells yes, you are."

Ten sashayed out of the bar to the sound of catcalls and whistles from her friends and the amused stares of the other patrons. Max, the regular afternoon musician and dear friend, quickly accompanied her strut with Roy Orbison's Pretty Woman. She blew him a kiss and stepped out into the sunlight.

Six to ten months. At best.

Why had she hid the news from her friends? The whole ride over, she'd rehearsed what she'd say and imagined their reactions.

"Guys, I have terrible news."

They're expressions would turn fearful.

Margot would say, "My God, Ten honey, what is it?"

Carlos and Lucy would grab one another's hands.

"It's—I have a brain tumor, and I only have six months to live."

All three would wail and cry. The waitress would bring them all free drinks and the owner would tell her, "Drinks on the house, for life," before bursting into tears. Max would apologize for never asking her out, to which she'd smile with fondness and gratitude because no one had been able to turn his head since his wife passed away.

She'd gotten no further in her soap opera version of the scene. To continue would mean including her father in the imagining, and it became too emotional. Too *real*.

Only, it still didn't *feel* real. Ten felt perfectly fine. Maybe a slight headache from the daytime margaritas. Or could it be the tumor? Lucy said she looked *off*. What did that even mean?

"Harper?"

She spun around and had to shield her eyes from the sun. *You've got to be kidding me. Nick fricking Keller? Him? Today of all days?* "Keller? What—what are *you* doing here?"

Nick Keller, her father's unauthorized biographer and all-round jerkface, walked toward her. As usual, his hair was too perfectly tousled by the breeze, his teeth too white, and his manner too easy.

He cast his arms wide, tilted his head in what he probably thought charming, and chuckled, "Public beach, sweetheart."

"Actually, *private* beach. For Cappy's patrons."

Ten turned away. She had nothing to say to Nick the Dick.

"So, do you still call me Nick the Dick?"

"Yup. You still writing books about people without their permission?"

"Yup." Nick softened his tone. "Come on, Harper. It's been five years. Did you even read it?"

"Nope. Never will, either."

"Jesus, Harper. There's nothing bad in it. Your Dad's a great guy. He's a *legend*. I loved him. That's why I wrote a book about his life. Not because I wanted to expose your family secrets. And I had his permission, by the way. Saying 'Unauthorized' sells more."

"But you didn't have my permission, and you *did* expose our private business, *Keller*. You used me to get to him, and once you got what you wanted, you—" Tenley halted.

Everything shifted, then spun. Suddenly up became down. It felt akin to being on the deck of a ship rocked by a tidal wave.

I'm not ready yet.

"Whoa, hey. I got you," said Nick close to her ear. "Sit. Head down. Breathe. That's right. Just breathe through it. You drunk, Harper?" Unmistakable laughter in his voice.

"Fuck off, Keller. No, I'm not drunk. I—it's nothing." She reached into her bag and pulled out her car keys with a shaking hand.

Nick took the keys and dropped them back in her purse. "Easy, killer. I'd offer to drive you, but I've been day-drinking, too. Come on, I'll walk you back to your place."

"I don't need a babysitter, thanks." Ten stood and walked away. She wobbled, but kept going.

"Suit yourself. I'm just gonna follow along right behind you."

Never in a million years would she let him know she felt relieved to have the company—even if it was his. Her father had vertigo, so she knew almost instantly what happened to her. It was just as he'd described. Nausea and residual fear lingered, but hell if she'd let Nick Keller know it.

"Whatever. I'm just going to ignore you."

"All right, Harper. You do that."

After a few minutes, she said, "Don't you have some barely legal bimbo to get back to?"

"Thought you were ignoring me?"

Ten said nothing.

"No, Harper. I'm solo... *ish*. Have been for a while. How about you? Still dating beefcake boy?"

"Sure am. His name is Josh." She stopped and whipped around. "Wait, how did you know—"

"You're not exactly a low-key kind of woman, Harper. Hell, you're a local celebrity around here." He spread his hands as if framing a billboard. "The wild, free-spirit, golden-haired Goddess of Pinellas County. The one, the only, Tenley Harper."

Ten rolled her eyes and shoved his bare shoulder. His tan, lean but muscular shoulder. She'd never noticed that before. Her inner monologue voice fake-sneezed the word *bullshit*.

Pushing the thoughts from her mind, she said, "More like, *daughter* of local celebrity, five-time World Wrestling Champion, Charlie 'The Hurricane' Harper,' you mean."

"Eh, Charlie's a legend, sure. But you? You're who everybody's watching. Come on, like you don't see how people look at you? Those three tagalongs of yours, they still hang on your every word?"

Ten blinked at him, bemused. Then, realizing he'd been referring to her friends, scowled. "They don't *hang on my every word*, Keller. They're my friends."

Nick scoffed, "Sure they are, Harper. *Fairweather* friends. If the shit hit the fan, they'd leave you high and dry, I bet."

A nerve sang. Nick Keller just spoke her fear. *That* was why Ten didn't tell them about the brain tumor. She feared they'd bail on her.

"Shut up, Keller."

He chuckled and whistled. After a few more minutes, he said, "How *is* your Dad these days?"

Ten almost didn't answer. But she remembered Charlie's fondness for Nick. The two men had bonded over cigars and wrestling nostalgia, and her father's affection for the man who told the world their life story never diminished, even after the book published. *Eye of the Hurricane, The Life and Legacy of Charlie 'The Hurricane' Harper*. Sixteen weeks on the New York Times Best Seller's list. For the cover, Nick used one of Charlie's press junket photos from the eighties, when he was built like a Mack truck and had long, shaggy, strawberry-blond hair and a San Tropez tan.

"Good days and bad," said Ten. "The tremors were getting bad until his new medication."

"I suppose you won't tell him hello for me? Or that—"

"Why'd you do it, Nick? Why did you sell my father out?"

Nick stopped and swore up at the sky. "Jesus Fucking Christ, Harper. I *didn't* sell him out, or you, or your family. He gave me permission. *I've* told you this. *Charlie* told you. Just read the damn book and you'll see for yourself."

Ten spun around, eyes ablaze. "You gained his trust—*my* trust—and then you conned him into telling you everything about our lives. Then, once the book published, you disappeared. What, was that just a coincidence? Oh, and I read more than enough, thank you."

"Then you see—"

Ten recited from memory, "*The Hurricane's only child should've been monikered after her father. Tenley Rose Harper has all the makings of a celebrity wild child, and no inclination to ever grow up. One could lay blame at her unconventional upbringing— growing up on the road, burly wrestlers for babysitters, the lack of a mother's guidance...* Does that ring any bells, Keller?"

"Tell me you kept reading, Harper." Nick's head dropped to his chest.

"Why, so I could learn all about what a motherless flake I am? Not interested."

"Harper, if you just—"

"Save it, Keller. We're here. You've done your good deed for the decade, now go stalk someone else."

Ten left him on the sidewalk—his hands on his hips and an exasperated expression on his face— and went inside the house. *The nerve.* Like *he* had any right to be exasperated by *her*. Asshole. Extremely good-looking asshole. She squeezed her eyes shut against the unbidden image of his tan, shirtless torso. He wasn't bodybuilder ripped like Josh. Nick was actually a little closer to a 'dad-bod' than a fitness model. Like he used to work out but didn't have time anymore.

"Why am I wasting a precious moment of my time thinking about that idiot?"

"What idiot?"

Ten jumped. "Jesus, Kablooey. You scared the shit out of me. Where's Dad?"

"Language, kid. Charlie's out on the lanai. I gotta check on the new kid at the gym. Coming by later? Loverboy moped around this morning. You have anything to do with that?"

Ten shrugged at her father's long-time trainer, manager, and best friend, Louis 'Louie Kablooey' Tamatoa. Louie's wresting career was on the rise when a serious back injury ended his climb. Charlie was ringside when it happened.

From his hospital bed, he'd asked Charlie, "If I can't be a wrestler no more, then what the hell am I gonna do, man?"

Charlie had said, "You'll be my manager. No one knows this business like you."

Between them, they had forty years of friendship, three ex-wives, four gyms, and now her dad's Parkinson's. Where some people may have backed away, Louis Tamatoa doubled down. When Ten got word of her father's diagnosis, Kablooey was the first person she told. The next week, he hired a full-time manager at the gym so he could help Charlie and Ten. That happened six years ago and Kablooey showed no signs of throwing in the towel.

"Listen, sweetheart. You know I'm not one to butt in on your personal life—"

"Bloo, you and Charlie had background checks done on everyone I've ever dated. You once put a guy in a headlock for beeping the horn instead of coming to the front door. Oh, and how about the time you—"

"Never mind any of that. All I'm sayin' is, you gotta either cut em loose, or commit. Don't you want to settle down, get married, and—"

"I'm perfectly happy the way things are. But thank you, Kablooey. I love you. Now go."

"All right, all right. Love you, too. Fitz and Lizzy are with your pops out back."

Ten kissed her surrogate uncle's cheek and thanked him. When the door clicked shut behind him, her smile fell, and she once again found herself alone with her thoughts. And fears. Her brain had yet to wrap around this new reality. There were things she should do, weren't there? A will to draw up, affairs to get in order. She had to tell someone; it was unavoidable. But who? Not her father. The news would be too hard for him. Losing his only child would be... she couldn't bear to think of it. No parent should out-live their child.

The threat of tears stung Ten's eyes, so she pushed the thought away. She would deal with this later, not right now. *Later*, she would figure it all out. Right *now*, she needed to get outside see her dad and her dogs and pretend everything was normal.

Before she could even make it down the hall, the front door opened again and Kablooey's voice broke the silence.

"Hey, you uh, know there's a guy out here for you, right? I think it's the guy that wrote the book. He's just sitting there on the curb."

Ten growled. "What the hell is he doing out there still? I told him to leave."

"You want for me to get rid him? I can escort him off the property. It would be my pleasure."

Ten considered the offer for a moment. A seventy-year-old man physically removing Nick Keller from her property seemed almost too much to pass up. Alas, she resisted the temptation and said, "No, just ignore him. He'll go away eventually. Or die of heatstroke, whichever comes first."

Kablooey shrugged, "Whatever you say."

Ten resisted the urge to peek out the window at Nick Keller and instead strode down the hall to the French doors that lead to the lanai and—further out—the beach. Fitz galloped to her on his long, gangly, Great Dane legs with little Lizzie close behind. She greeted them with matching enthusiasm and called out hello to her father.

Charlie sat in a lounge chair facing the ocean. He watched the late day sun sink towards the horizon, but turned his head slowly towards his daughter, a faint smile on his lips.

"Hi, Daddy. Can I get you anything?"

"Just the company of my beautiful daughter is enough for me."

Ten settled beside him, the dogs following close behind. As soon as she sat in the chair, they took up their usual positions. Lizzie hopped onto her father's lap, and Fitz sprawled by Ten's feet. They sat like this for a while, neither speaking, both staring out at the waves. Charlie stroked Lizzie's soft pate; his hand tremored only mildly. It was a good day.

"So, what adventures has my darling daughter been up to today?"

"Oh, you know, the usual. Drinks with Lucy, Margot, and Carlos. Took a stroll along the beach. That's about it, I think."

"No, I thought you had something else to do today. An appointment, wasn't it?"

The moment presented itself. She could tell him right now, or she could let him have peace for a while longer. She decided on silence. Maybe for cowardice, maybe protectiveness, but either way she let the moment pass.

"Nothing important, just an annual physical."

"Eh, my girl is as healthy as a horse. Just like her dad. Until I…"

Ten leaned over and patted her dad's knee. "You're still strong like bull, Dad."

Barrel-chested and straight-backed, The Hurricane could still take an opponent out with an armbar or a takedown. Maybe even a full Nelson. Not a slam or fireman's carry though. She side-glanced her father.

"Dad? You think you could still do a slam?"

"You callin' me a stiff? Stand up and I'll show you," he growled, using his best Hurricane Harper voice.

Ten giggled just like when she was a child. "I believe you, never mind."

More seriously, he asked, "The Josh kid need an ass-kicking? Someone else? I can round up the boys and we'll take him to the mat."

Laughing again, she said, "After more than twenty years of being on the road with you and the boys, I think I can handle any heel that tries to get funny. Don't worry about me, Daddy."

"Atta girl."

Truer words couldn't have been spoken. Ten spent as much time in the ring as she did in the back offices with tutors and sitters. At age four, Ten practiced arm bars and leg locks on her dolls instead of dressing them up. At nine, she could backflip off the middle rope turnbuckle. Technically, she could do it from the top rope, but Charlie wouldn't let her until she turned twelve. When she turned sixteen, she helped the booker, Marty Coughlin, with scripts, and at nineteen she wrote them herself *and* got credit.

When on break or off on injury, their beach house turned into a mecca for wrestlers and their families. Charlie welcomed everyone, whether they were a Face or a Heel, Green or a Draw, it didn't matter. He had only two rules. No juicing around 'the kid' and act right. No one needed to ask what he meant. Act right encompassed everything one would expect—they watched their mouth, kept their beefs quiet, and the drugs off his property. Oh, and never mess with his daughter.

Only the only time—that she knew of—someone broke the rules. Tony 'The Golden Boy' Starling found out just how serious Charlie was about his rules. The twenty-four-year old had risen as their up and coming Face and Charlie had taken a shine to him, putting Tony under his wing and showing him the ropes. Ten had just turned seventeen and she fell head over heels for the hulking blonde Adonis the moment she saw him.

Tony made a great show of respect for Charlie, never even glancing in Ten's direction when his mentor was around. But when he wasn't around, it became another story. In retrospect, it seemed almost inevitable, really. Charlie let the young man stay in the guest house, a mere fifty yards from the main house where Ten lived. Charlie still toured and promoted on occasion, and she'd been old enough to not have to go with him all the time.

A few 'accidental' meetings by the pool led to walks on the beach, which led to a brief fling. Ten had no idea about his other flings or the girl he impregnated six months prior, *or* the cocaine habit that steadily ate both a hole in his nose and his pockets.

All she knew was that she loved him. He told her he loved her, too, but they had to keep things quiet for the sake of his career. As part of the grooming for making him the new Face, she readily agreed, knowing that the script called for him to be 'swoon-worthy' and available.

The W.C.A. wanted to draw more of a female audience, and Tony appeared to be their ticket to do so. His appearances already created a buzz, but they had to phase out the current script featuring the feud between Buzzsaw Bobby and Mr. Mayhem before bringing forward Tony.

Plus, they had behind the scenes drama. Management wanted to use Charlie's mentorship in the script, but with a twist. They wanted The Hurricane to turn Heel, something Charlie opposed vehemently. Ten overheard the heated conversation between her father and W.C.A. owner, Jason Kilroy.

"I'm telling you, Charlie, it'll be great. A whole new life to your career, buddy."

"Jack, I'm telling *you*, I don't like it. I told you last year, I'm ready to retire, man. I haven't been feeling right, and shit, I'm tired. Let me go out on top, will ya? I don't want to go out a Heel."

"Buddy, come on, now. You haven't been a Heel since, what? Nineteen-eight-seven? This could be a whole new era for you. Think of the merch."

"It was eighty-eight. It was the fucking pits, man. I had little kids throwing shit at me in the grocery store and calling me names. I had a woman follow me out of the movie theater once and berate me for disappointing her son. Then—"

"I hear you, buddy, I do. Let's not rush into a decision, okay? Sit on it for a few weeks. We got time. How's the kid doing? He seem like he's got his shit together?"

"Yeah, he's good. Nothing I can't handle. Jason, man, I won't change my mind on this."

"We'll see, Charlie. We'll see."

Tony inadvertently decided for them. When Charlie came off tour, he could tell that something had changed. He could smell it in the air, he told Ten much later. Neither acted any different, they behaved as if they were mere acquaintances in front of him. That was their mistake.

"How can that be," he'd wondered aloud to Kablooey one afternoon at the gym.

"What do you mean?"

"I mean he lives in our guesthouse. They see each other almost every day. But they never talk to one another? I asked her when I got back how everything went. You know what she said?"

"Five more. Push. No what's she say?"

"She said, 'How would I know?' All defensive-like. I mean, what's with that?"

"Legs now. Two sets of twelve. Well, she *is* a teenager, Charlie. And a *girl*. Bound to happen. Don't freak out about it. She's got a crush, is all. Tony knows the deal. Off-limits. He'd be a fucking moron to screw this up."

"He's twenty-four. He's juicing like a mother fucker. He ain't too bright, Bloo. I just hope he's not so stupid to think I won't bury him."

"Well, if he's messing with our girl, you can bet I'll help you do it, too."

Charlie watched them like a hawk the following week. On the surface there was nothing to see. It wasn't until the following Thursday, one a.m. He's been having a hard time sleeping, so he walked down to the beach. It was a near-full moon, so Charlie hadn't needed to turn on the outside lights to illuminate his way. It was a good thing, otherwise, he might have missed what he saw next.

Charlie had just lifted the latch when movement at the water's edge caught his eye. Squinting, he made out two figures. He could they were a man and a woman; their outlines gave them away. As he watched, the taller figure bent down and kissed his companion, dipping her back. Long hair fanned out behind her.

Son of a bitch.

He'd seen enough. He jerked the gate open and stormed toward the couple, shouting Ten's name. Only when he reached the two did he realize that the woman was not his daughter, but a stranger with Tony.

"Charlie," stammered Tony, trying to sound relaxed, "scared the daylights out of me, man. This is my, uh, friend Chantelle. Chantelle, this is the one and only Hurricane Harper."

From behind Charlie came another voice. "Dad? Tony? What's —"

Ten looked from Tony to the woman, to her father. The confusion in her face quickly turned to dismay, then horror. With a cry, she covered her mouth and bolted back to the house.

"Ten, wait, I —"

"Pack up your shit, boy. You better be off my property before I get up in the morning."

"Charlie, it's not what you —"

Charlie took several menacing steps towards Tony. The younger man put his hands up and said, "Sorry sir, I'll—I never meant for any of this —"

Charlie waved him off in disgust and followed his daughter back to the house, leaving Tony and the now very confused young woman behind. That was the last time Charlie saw Tony outside of the ring.

"Sweetheart? Open up, it's Dad."

"Go away. I don't want to talk."

Charlie waited a moment, unsure what to do next. He half wanted to strangle her for getting involved with a wrestler. She knew better. How could she not know better? Then he cursed himself. *He* should've known better. These kinds of people were all she ever knew. It was only natural she would gravitate towards them. He should have sent her to a private school, or public school, at least. It wasn't like Charlie hadn't been warned about raising a daughter in that environment. But after the business with her mother—well, he couldn't bear to not have her close by. Nor could he afford to give up the money he made.

"I'll be in the kitchen."

If anything could pull her from her room, it would be Charlie's famous chocolate chip and banana pancakes. He gathered the ingredients and cooked and waited. Twenty minutes later, Ten pulled out a chair across from him and sat, keeping her head down and her eyes on the table. From the brief glimpse he caught of her face when she walked in, he knew she'd been crying. He had half a mind to walk to the guesthouse put Golden Boy through a wall.

Instead, he set down a plate before her, then a tall glass of milk. He made the same arrangement for himself and sat down. They ate in silence, quite enough to hear the waves crashing outside. And the rev of an engine. Tony's, no doubt. Charlie kept his head down to his plate but cast his eyes up at his daughter. Her fork hovered over her plate and then she dropped it with a clang.

"Say it, Daddy."

Charlie's breath whistled in and out through his nose, trying to remain calm. He wanted to say all the things she expected him to say. He wanted to say, *what were you thinking*? He wanted to say, *how could you*? But the sight of her quivering chin silenced those admonishments.

"I'm sorry he turned out to be a shit head."

A laugh that could've just as easily been a cough burst from Ten's throat.

"He's a shit head all right." She looked up at her father, forlorn and contrite, and said, "I'm sorry, Daddy. I should've known better."

Charlie nodded once. "Yup, you should've. What's done is done, though. Now what are we gonna do about it?"

A wicked gleam flickered in both pairs of green eyes. Ten grinned. "Marty has given me free reign on the booking with this one, as long as the bosses don't hear about it. "

"That's a lot of workers to get on board, kiddo."

Ten shrugged. "You let me worry about that, and you just do your part."

Charlie raised his milk glass to his daughter, and she raised hers. Jason Kilroy would get his Heel. It just would not be the one he expected. That night Ten worked extra hard on the script. By her hand, there'd be no quick burn for the Golden Boy. It would be slow, painful, and gratifying. For the Harpers, that is.

Hard to believe nineteen years had passed since then. The last they heard about Tony he'd done hard time for armed robbery. It made a brief splash in tabloid news. But like those things do, it faded back into the recesses of people's memories, affording nothing more than a brief, 'I think I kind of remember him,' before moving on with life. She'd felt a pang of pity, then guilt, which she expressed to her father.

He'd reminded her that Tony Starling had put himself on a self-destructive path well before and after he tangled with the Harpers. He was a grown man who had to live with his choices in life, just like everyone else. The opportunity of a lifetime in his lap, and all he'd taken away from it was a nasty drug habit.

Ten took away from the experience an understanding of how easily emotions could overrule sensibilities. To let attractive packaging blind oneself to the contents... or lack thereof. She vowed to never be that gullible again. Tenley Harper called the shots in her romantic life, no one else. Or at least, she used to. She supposed her future romances *had* no future, since she'd be gone in a matter of months.

Don't think about that now.

Speaking of romances, she supposed she would have to deal with the Josh situation. Kablooey was right, she needed to cut the poor boy loose. He'd been such fun, too. A shame. She never thought he would get attached, a man with so many options, so many younger women fawning and falling all over him.

Wasn't that the way of it, though? People always want what they can't have. Take Ten. She wanted more time, and it was the one thing she'd almost run out of. The knowledge remained too surreal to fathom.

⁷ NICK

Nick Keller sat on the curb outside of Tenley's house and threw pebbles and seashell fragments into the road. Something she'd said earlier nagged at him. To be fair, almost everything she said nagged at him, but he swatted those petty attacks away like pesky flies.

It was the thing she *hadn't* directed at him, but to herself, that echoed in his brain.

I'm not ready yet.

Those were her words outside Cappy's. Did she think she was dying or something? And *why* would she think that?

The urge to pound on her door and ask her directly conflicted with the one that told him to walk away and not look back. Literally and figuratively.

Unbeknownst to Tenley Harper, Nick had been keeping tabs on the little nymph.

Nymph. Where did that come from, Keller?

No use playing stupid. He knew where the term originated. And why. He had a crush on her. A crush that began six years ago, when she answered the same door in some crazy gauzy outfit that exposed most of her body. She had flowers braided into her long wavy hair and almost no makeup on, and her feet were bare.

Ten had tilted her head and smiled. "Can I help you?"

"I—you… is this Charlie Harper's house?"

Her smile had dropped, and her expression became guarded. "Who wants to know? Listen, if you're another asshole from the tabloids, you're gonna have to go fuck yourself."

As she closed the door on Nick, he pleaded with her to just listen. Through the crack, she looked him up and down, then glanced around the street. Presumably looking for a news van or paparazzi.

"I'm not here to ask about your Dad's Parkinson's. It's a shit deal that someone sold him out and blabbed to the tabloids. I'm a writer, Miss—"

Ten, still wary, said "Harper. I'm his daughter."

Instinct made him feign an oblivious air when she'd opened the door, but Nick recognized her. How could he not, given her status as one of Pinellas County's handful of resident celebrities? Unlike other children-of-celebrity brats, though, Tenley Harper lived the way she did not *because* of the notoriety of being The Hurricane's daughter, but despite it. He had to tread lightly around her.

"Of course. A-anyhow. I've been a fan of your Dad's since I was a kid and I'd love to write a book about him. Could I talk with him?"

"Sorry, but I don't think that'd be a good—"

"Ten? Who's at the door?"

Charlie came up behind his daughter, dwarfing her and filling the whole door frame.

"It's no one, Dad. He's just leaving." Ten gave Nick a pointed, *get the fuck out of here* glare.

Nick ignored her. "Sir? My name's Nick Keller. I'm a writer and I'd love to write about your life story. I think a lot of people would enjoy learning more about the greatest pro wrestler that ever lived. What do you say?"

Charlie stared hard at Nick long enough to make him squirm and fear he'd be physically thrown off the property. Ten looked as if she expected the same, although with an expression that bore more enthusiasm than Nick liked. Then the towering giant laughed.

"Let him in, sweetheart. If we don't like him, we'll feed him to the alligators out back."

"Daddy, I don't—"

"It's fine, pumpkin. Don't worry," said Charlie.

He patted her cheek with affection and Tenley took his hand in both of hers and nodded. It served as Nick's first glimpse at the extraordinary bond the two shared. It touched him.

As he learned more about Charlie, the enigma that was Tenley Harper became no less paradoxical. No matter how much Nick insinuated himself into the Harper's life, he could never get past the glacial air she reserved for just him. A truth even Charlie acknowledged.

Charlie chuckled after one cold greeting from Ten. "Son, I wish I could say she's like that with everyone, but I'm afraid it's just you. She doesn't like you, not one bit."

Nick tried to take it in stride, but it irked him to no end, and he found he couldn't stop from provoking her any chance he got. It was easy getting under skin. Hell, all he had to do was *breathe* near her to raise her hackles.

Meanwhile, he mused and puzzled over his personal Ten conundrum as much as he did her public life. Somehow, she managed to be both audacious *and* private. Her Boho-Chic style, her cascades of ocean air tousled tresses, and her easy smile drew people to her with a magnetic pull. And though she never pursued fame outside of what was thrust upon her, photographers still cropped up to take her pictures when she strolled the streets with her hodge-podge dog menagerie or her friends.

What struck Nick about her now was the same as when he'd first saw her face more than twenty years earlier. That time, a television tube—he in his parent's living room, she on the interview set of the W.C.A—and hundreds of miles had separated them. After some digging, then a 'duh' moment, Nick found that one interview with Tenley again on YouTube.

At fourteen, Ten was already a beauty. Nick, fifteen at the time, felt like someone had knocked the wind out of him as he watched Vance Vincent, a local news channel host, interview her in a special broadcast before the stadium match in Nick's town.

The fifteen-year old wrestling enthusiast sat glued to the T.V. set, anticipating seeing all his favorites. The preview promised interviews with Jimmy the Snake, Jonny 'Mr. Amazing' Armstrong, and the one and only Hurricane Harper. So, when Vance talked about a 'special young guest' that few people knew anything about, young Nick groaned in annoyance.

"Just get to the wrestlers," said Nick to the television.

Onscreen, Vance said, "All right, lets meet the extraordinary young lady who's actually grown up behind the scenes and up close to the super stars of the Wrestling Champions of America, Miss Tenley Harper. Yes, that's right, folks, you heard me. *Harper*, as in world champ, Charlie the Hurricane Harper's daughter."

Nick sat forward. *No fair. She got to grow up around these guys?* Then, the most beautiful girl he'd ever seen walked onto the set and sat cross-legged on the chair across from Vance. Tenley Harper looked like no girl Nick knew. Blonde hair flowed wild and sun-kissed and fell in waves over her shoulders and nearly to her waist. Her body was tan, lean and strong looking, like a dancer or a gymnast. Her full mouth stayed in a straight line, neither smiling nor frowning. Then those green eyes pierced through the camera, straight through Nick's heart. She spoke.

"Hello, Mr. Vincent. Thank you for having me on your show."

Nick caught himself grinning like an idiot. Even her voice was unexpected. Low, almost hoarse sounding, like she'd been yelling the night before. Considering she probably spent many nights ringside, it was possible, even likely. Again, a wave of envy flooded Nick's senses. What he wouldn't give to live a day in Tenley Harper's shoes. In Tenley Harper's *life*.

As a fifteen-year-old hormonal boy, all Nick only focused on her looks. He scarcely registered anything said in the interview. As a grown man re-watching it, he tuned in to her words and mannerisms. Her composure struck him, both back then and later. Ten hadn't fidgeted or giggled, or twirled her hair, or even use any of the slang popular in the eighties. There were no exclamations of 'like' or 'totally' breaking up each sentence. She answered each question with sparse, concise language.

"So, Tenley, tell me—tell the world watching— what it's like growing up in the wild and crazy world of wresting."

"It's fun, mostly. We're a family."

"A family," repeated Vance. "An unconventional family, though, right?"

"Yes," said Ten. She stared at him, her expression placid.

Vance waited for her to elaborate. When she didn't, he coughed and shifted in his seat. "Ah, how so? What makes your... family unconventional?"

"Well, that's your word for it. Not mine. It's normal for me. I have schoolwork and a curfew. I can watch an R rated movie as long as my Dad watches it first. So, I think that's what other kids do, too."

"Sure, sure," said Vance looking first at Ten then into the camera with exaggerated incredulity. "But isn't it odd that everyone around you has names like, Jimmy the Snake and The Destroyer? How does your mom provide balance to all of that?"

"I don't have—"

"Hey there, sweetheart," said Hurricane Harper as his massive body filled the screen.

His appearance on camera seemed unscripted. He took Vance Vincent's considerably smaller hand in his and shook it. There was such a cold, glint in his eyes as they bore into the smaller man.

"Nice to meet you, Mr. Vincent. Hope you don't mind my joining my little girl out here."

"No—I not at all. I was just asking her about—"

"Vance, I came out to offer your viewers a chance to win front row seats to tonight's match. That all right with you, friend?"

Vance faced the camera and said, "Folks, when Hurricane Harper wants to do something, who am I so tell him no?"

The exchange, Nick realized watching it for a second time and with the eyes of an adult, was tension filled. Vance had crossed a line, and whether he knew it beforehand, he certainly knew it then. Charlie sat next to his daughter and slunk one mammoth arm across the back of her chair and dwarfing her and the seat he filled. She smiled and leaned against his side and let him take over the rest of the interview.

As a teenage boy in the throngs of testosterone fueled behaviors, he pushed thoughts of the feral looking girl to the recesses of his mind to focus on the more tangible ones. But he never forgot her. It wasn't until a colleague at the Journal—also a former pro-wrestling fan in his youth—suggested he write a book about his one-time hero and all-time legend.

Nick insisted his interest lie solely in Charlie Harper's story, but the moment he saw Ten, and all grown up, he understood the truth. If he wasn't in love with the woman, it had to be something pretty damn close to it.

Nearly six years later and here he sat, burning his ass on the curb outside her house once again. What the fuck was wrong with him? He wasn't bad looking. He had financial security, made a good living as a writer, and considered himself reasonably intelligent. Nick wouldn't say he could get any woman he wanted—he wasn't a total dick—but he had no difficulties finding bedmates. Nines and tens, too. Not fives. He remembered with a groan that he left a nine-and-a-half on the beach to follow Tenley fricking Harper home.

"Yo, loverboy. She ain't coming back out, you know. Go home before you get heatstroke."

Nick looked over his shoulder. "Hey, Kablooey. Remember me? Nick Kel—"

"Yeah, yeah. I remember. I also remember Ten throwing a trophy at your head. You really pissed her off, kid."

Nick rubbed the phantom pain in the back of his skull where the marble edge of the trophy gouged him. "I sure did, Bloo. Hey, can I ask you... did *you* ever read the book?"

Kablooey shrugged and kept walking to his truck. "Yeah, some. It was okay."

"Gee, thanks."

"Go home, Keller. Tomorrow's a new day."

He waited until the truck rounded the corner, then stood. His ass stung. His ego didn't feel much better. He was down, but not defeated, though. Tenley Harper made him more determined than ever to win her esteem. Or at least her forgiveness. As for her love, he accepted the improbability. Grudgingly.

[8] KENNY

Kenny walked through the hallways of Conway T. Booker Middle School in a daze. The shouts and ruckus of boys and girls, the slamming of lockers, the fifth period bell all sounded far off and muted. He vaguely noticed a few students staring at him, their expressions showing a mild curiosity before sliding off him and onto more interesting objects.

Doug Pfeiffer, the English Composition teacher, called his name twice over the throng, then again a third time, eschewing the formal 'Mr. Harper' for his given name, something not done in front of the students. Much too familiar and casual. Kenny ignored him, making a mental note to admonish him—politely, of course—for such a breach, and kept walking. His pace, normally brisk and purposeful, slowed further. The final bell rang before he even made it halfway to his classroom.

The students, already in the room behind the closed door, were at the volume and activity level typical of a class without adult supervision. Or when a substitute taught. Kenny's hand hovered above the doorknob. Ahead, at the end of the hall, sat the heavy metal double doors with the spring bar handles and caged windows. The sun poured through, blinding him. Kenny shielded his eyes and squinted.

What am I doing?

With no thought to consequence—or at least little thought—Kenny James Harper continued his trance-like trek down the rest of the corridor, out the school doors, and into the blinding sunlight.

"Kenny? What are you doing out here? Aren't you in class?"

Kenny blinked at Jim Parsons, the head custodian. "I-I'm going to get my wife back."

Jim cocked his head and scratched his chin. "Well, have at it, chief."

Kenny said nothing more to Jim, but to himself, he repeated, "I'm going to get my wife back," as he walked—no *strode*—to his car. He had a purpose if not a plan, and for the moment, it was enough. His first stop would be home. Perhaps he'd find Lee there, and he could stop her. He rehearsed aloud what he'd say.

"Lee, we have a good life. It is highly implausible at this stage to—no, that's not it."

He drummed his fingers on the steering wheel and thought.

"Lee, we have a successful marriage that has withstood—" Kenny stopped again.

It wouldn't do to bring up their difficulties. Doing so might further her resolve. No, he needed to remind her of the good times, the fun, the laughs. That shouldn't be hard to do. *Laughs. Fun. Good times. Think, Kenny, think*. The chirp and whoop of a police siren startled him. His rearview mirror revealed a black and white cruiser, its blue and red lights spinning. His sideview mirror showed the approach of a uniformed sheriff. A glance out his windshield informed Kenny that he'd stopped at a green light. He powered down his window.

"He-hello, Sheriff."

"Good afternoon, sir. Do you realize you're stopped at a green light?"

"No, well, yes, I-I do now. I didn't before."

"Mhm. License and registration, please."

"Yes, yes, of course."

Kenny fumbled in the glove compartment, found the required paperwork, and handled it to the unsmiling policeman.

"License, too."

"Right, duh," said Kenny with a laugh. The sheriff did not join in.

After reaching in the pocket he normally kept his wallet and finding it empty, he tried the other, darting apologetic smiles out the window. Strange. He knew he had it in the morning, and when he stopped home for lunch. Dismayed, Kenny realized where it sat—the downstairs bathroom. He'd used the toilet—as per his routine, since he didn't like to move his bowels at work—and set his wallet on top of the tank.

He did this every time, and every time he remembered to put his wallet back into his pants pocket after drying his hands. Except for this time. *This* time the news of his wife's intention to leave him—effective immediately—distracted him.

"Sir?"

Kenny, in recalling the series of events that had rendered him wallet-less at the most inopportune time, had sat frozen, hand hovering waist-high. He craned his neck and offered a wan smile.

"Sir, I'm going to have to ask you to step out of the vehicle."

"Oh, but that's wholly unnecessary, Sheriff. I just—"

"Are you refusing to step out of the vehicle?"

"No, I-I just don't think it's a necessary step. I live up the street, and my wallet is at home. On top of the toilet tank. I prefer to use the toilet at home, and well, my wife is leaving me, so you see the error, I'm sure."

The sheriff stared at him a moment. "Sir, have you been drinking?"

"Drinking? In the middle of the day? Don't be absurd."

His contempt for the notion made him forget who he addressed. It would seem calling an officer of the law absurd was frowned upon, because the next thing Kenny knew, he found himself handcuffed and in the back of the cruiser. After further introspection, Kenny realized it was less the tone he'd used and more to do with the unfortunate timing of his arm grab.

He tried to explain once again when the sheriff entered the cruiser to presumably transport Kenny to the police station.

"Sheriff, I was merely trying to get your attention. You'd have seen, had you not turned to speak into your walkie-talkie thing, that I reached for your *arm*, not your *gun*."

The policeman, now thoroughly vexed, met his eyes in the rearview mirror and made a contemptuous sound, then said, "If I had a dime for every time I heard *that*."

Kenny doubted the man encountered as frequent gun grabs as he implied. He knew the crime rate statistics of Dunedin, and types of crimes committed, so unless he'd come from a different, more crime infested county, the odds were against such implications. Kenny stayed silent on the matter. It would all get sorted out quickly enough, he was confident. Confident-*ish*. He'd just call Lee and she'd—*would* she come to the station to help him? Surely, for something like this she would.

Lee always handled the complicated matters. Not that this situation was complicated—it was rather straight forward once explained—and she'd only have to post bail. Regardless, Lee would know just what to say to make everything right again. Even after the miscarriages—all four of them—she had been the stoic one, the pragmatic one. Kenny had blubbered like a fool after the first two, less so each subsequent. He'd gone sheet-white at the sight of the needles she'd jabbed herself with regularity for their invitro procedures.

It went for the mundane, as well. When the cable company overcharged them, or the refrigerator repair man failed to fix the problem but charged them anyhow, Lee set them straight. If something rang up wrong in the store, Lee had the manager over right quick to fix it. She ran her classroom and their household with almost military precision.

In his head, Kenny listed all the things his wife did. Shopped and prepared their meals. Washed, folded and put away their laundry. Changed the bed sheets weekly, took Dexter for his vet appointments and gave him his medicine, managed the bills and the annual homeowner tasks of calling the furnace guy and the chimney sweep company. There was more, but what he'd remembered caused him considerable dismay. What did *he* do, besides bring home a paycheck and dry the dishes?

"Hey sweetie, what are *you* in for?"

A tall, elegant woman in a sequined spaghetti-strapped gown in an eye-catching shade of purple sat down beside Kenny. Her hair was platinum-blonde and huge. It made Kenny think of Dolly Parton. The woman wore an excessive amount of makeup and perfume, but the former looked flawless and the latter smelled nice. Kenny's confusion veered from the vague to the complete.

"This is a co-ed jail cell?"

The Dolly Parton woman stared at him a moment, then tossed her head back and laughed. Her teeth were also perfect. The laugh sounded deep, throaty. Kenny smiled, not following. When her laughter died down, she reassessed Kenny's blank expression.

"Oh, honey." Dolly-not-Dolly put a hand on Kenny's knee and leaned in close. "Sweetie, no, this is not a... co-ed jail."

"But then, why are you—oh, I see now. You're a—"

"Performance artist, darling. Fuchsia Featherbottom, at your service." She... he extended his hand, palm and fingertips down.

"I-Kenny Harper, how do you do." He shook the proffered hand awkwardly, which made Fuchsia laugh again. "Fuchsia—like your dress, right?"

The exotic man-woman did a shoulder roll reminiscent of Marilyn Monroe. "More like the other way around. First came the name, then came the dress. We put on a hell of a show down at La Rue on Wednesday nights. You should come see us. First drink is on moi."

"Oh, well, that is very nice of you, Fuchsia. I-I may just take you up on that. I'm sure it's a delightful show. But, if you're show is on Wednesday nights, why are you all dressed up today? It's Thursday, you know."

Fuchsia Featherbottom lost the feminine voice. "Long story short, I got hungry after I left work last night and stopped for some fast food—terrible choice, I know—and some bozo got a little frisky in line. Normally, I don't get too upset, but I was tired and hungry. Hell, sweetie, I was *hangry*. So, I decked him. Knocked him out cold, and didn't even break a nail, thank you very much." Fuchsia studied her long sparkly nails with a satisfied smirk.

"And they arrested you?"

"Yep, *and* the barbarian. He already posted bail."

"I'm sorry that happened to you, Fuchsia."

"Thanks, honey. Now, your turn. Fess up, what'd a nice man like you do?"

"Oh, well, it's all just a misunderstanding. You see, I stopped at a green light—"

"Problem number one, honey."

"And the sheriff mistakenly thought I tried to grab his gun. Oh, and I don't have my license."

"You had me at 'grabbed an officer of the law's gun.' Child, what were you even *thinking*?"

Kenny, after a momentary hesitation followed by the realization they both had nothing better to do than to share their stories, told Fuchsia Featherbotter—AKA Frank Tropher, Kenny learned—his life story leading up to his wife of over fifteen years leaving him without warning.

"So, let me get this straight. Your wife thought she had a brain tumor, went to the doctor and found out she was right as rain, and then said see ya, wouldn't wanna be ya? Over the phone, no less? Damn, that's *harsh*. Not for nothing, baby, but you might be better off."

Kenny blanched. He didn't want a stranger to have that kind of impression of Lee.

"No, I mean yes, but there's more to it. I'm certain now it's all my fault. I've just been thinking of all Lee has done and all she's gone through the years."

He chronicled everything in Lee's life—from her younger brother passing away at an early age, to then her parents passing away when she was still in her teens onto the infertility problems and the miscarriages. "After all of that, Lee still took care of everything. Took care of *me*."

"Ah, I see. The old taken for granted for too long syndrome," said Fuchsia with a sage expression.

"Is that... a thing?"

Kenny's new friend laughed, but he could tell it wasn't meant to be mocking. "Yes, you could say that. Tale as old as time, sweetie. So, what are you going to do about it?"

"Well," said Kenny, scratching his chin, "I'm going to ask her to come back home."

"Yes, yes. But how are you going to win her back? What are you going to *say*, Kenny baby?"

'I-I'll remind her we've invested over fifteen years into this marriage. W-we have a home, and careers, and there's Dexter to think—"

"Yawn, yawn, *yawn*," said Fuchsia, who then emphasized with an exaggerated yawn. "Honey, that sounded like you're reading off the back of a cereal box. You are not going win that woman back like *that*, trust me."

"Oh. So, what would you do if you were trying to win back the love of *your* life?"

"There's a good start right there. *Love of your life*. That's what a woman wants to hear. You listen to Fuchsia, okay? Tell her she's the best thing that ever happened to you. Let her know you'd be *nothing* without her. Say you'd be *lost* without her. Then do something romantic, but manly. Women don't want a sad sap. Be assertive. And honey? Wear something more... modern. Lose the glasses and the pocket protector. Get a haircut from this decade."

Kenny glanced down at his slacks and button-down, short-sleeved dress shirt. He had six pairs and the same number of shirts—in beige, dark blue, light blue, and three white—in his side of the bedroom closet. Phil the barber had been trimming his thick, slightly wavy hair for ten years. Just above the ears, parted to the left, precisely half an inch below his earlobes in the back. He owned contact lenses and wore them for kayaking and jogging, but his ultra-lightweight brown framed glasses were easier and more practical for everyday use.

Fuchsia continued. "Usually, I'd say, be the man she fell in love with, but honey, something tells me you haven't changed one *bit* since you met wifey. Am I right?"

Fuchsia's daddy long-legs eyelashes fluttered.

Kenny bristled and tried to come up with a list of ways he'd changed. "Sure, I have. I-I used to part my hair on the right. And I switched from teaching third grade to fifth. I stopped eating red meat. I—"

"Stop, please." Fuchsia's hand went up and his/her head dropped. "Okay, here's what I want you to do. Go see my girl Jacqui at Salon Halo on Main Street. Tell her Fuchsia sent you. Next door is a—God help me—GAP store. My friend Patrice works there, ask for her and tell her—"

"Fuchsia sent me?"

"Exactly. Tell her you want—hmm, let's see. Stand up a sec, honey. Turn around. Mhm. Got it. Tell her you want a cross between Ryan Gosling, The

Notebook and Pierce Bronson, Mama Mia. Can you remember all that?"

Kenny didn't know who those two men were, but he vaguely recalled Lee crying over a movie that had the work 'Notebook' in it. "I think so. Cameli Salon, and—"

"Oh, Lord. *Capelli* Salon. Then, the GAP to see…" Fuchsia stared at Kenny, nodding in encouragement.

Kenny said, "The GAP to see… Patrick."

Fuchsia fluttered those long lashes at him again. "Patrice. Pa-*trice*."

"Hey, you two. Bail's posted, Harper. Frank, you're free to go. Charges got dropped," said a tired looking sheriff as he slid open the steel gate.

"That creep dropped the charges? I can't believe it," said Fuchsia.

The sheriff shrugged, then smirked. "Guess he didn't want his buddies to know he got knocked out by a girl."

"But I'm not—"

"Or maybe it was on account of grabbing the ass of another man that persuaded him. Who knows?" He laughed and elaborated. "Deputy O'Shea saw the surveillance camera video. Informed the gentleman that it was a clear case of sexual harassment, assault even. Spelled out the situation to him, told him how it would play out, and here we are."

Kenny, listening to this, felt abashed by his preconceived idea of how the police would handle a person like Fuchsia Featherbottom. If he'd expected anything, it would've been condescension, not this display of empathy and compassion for someone who so clearly did not fit the norm. His surprise must have shown.

"Don't look so shocked, Harper. We got family, too." To Fuchsia he said, "My kid brother came out last month. O'Shea's cousin does what you do, too."

Fuchsia's chin quivered, and his voice wobbled when he said, "Just another reason to love a man in uniform, honey."

"Aw, come on, now. Let's get you two outta here."

Kenny said, "Does my wife seem mad?"

The sheriff called over his shoulder, "How would I know?"

"Isn't she out there?"

"Not unless she's six-four and goes by the name Chet."

Kenny groaned. He forgot that his second call had been to his older brother. Chet was normally the last person Kenny would call for help but dialing his parents, both in their eighties, with such alarming news—their son, arrested and in jail—wasn't an option. *Chet.* Kenny shuddered with dread. He heard him even before they came through the heavy doors into the station.

"So, I told her, 'Sweetheart, I don't care how you do it, just—well, hey *little* brother. Get a load a you. Mr. Goody Two Shoes, arrested. Nice job. Guys, my baby brother here slept with a night light until age eleven. Now he's assaulting officers of the law."

The handful of sheriffs and deputies laughed along with Chet. He wore his usual attire of cargo pants, USMC tight t-shirt, and fire department cap. Any moment, he would refer to either the fire department or his status as a retired United States Marine—never simply Marine. Chet mentioned one or both at an interval of every three to five sentences.

"Good thing I've got some connections through the fire department, little bro, otherwise you'd really be in it deep."

Reference one down. Kenny sighed, conscious of Fuchsia beside him and what he must think as his eyes traveled back and forth between him and Chet.

"Thanks Chet," said Kenny, his jaw tight and hands fisted in his pockets, "if you can just give me a lift to the impound, I'll be out of your hair."

"Speaking of hair, bro, your lid is not United States Marine Corps acceptable. You gotta go see my barber. He'll straighten your act out. At least your appearance."

Kenny opened his mouth to give his standard *thanks, but no thanks* response to Chet's frequent offers to help 'straighten him out,' but Fuchsia jumped in quicker.

"Marines, huh? Semper Fi."

Chet sputtered then scoffed. 'Pshtt, *you're* a Marine?"

Fuchsia smiled. "Combat vet, Iraq. You?"

Chet's face reddened and he mumbled something about Hawaii.

"Ah, well, we can all make it to the front lines, can we? Anyhow, Kenny is coming with me. *Right*, Kenny?"

Chet looked at Fuchsia with barley contained fury. Realizing he had all eyes on him, his facial expressions rearranged to display a myriad of emotions. Disbelief. Contempt. He settled on sardonic amusement.

"Made a new friend, huh, little bro?"

Kenny looked between the two men—one, the physical epitome of G.I. Joe, the other, the product of a lovechild between Marilyn Monroe and Rue Paul. Kenny felt a moment of satisfaction in remembering the famous drag queen's name. Then he shifted back to the conundrum of which person he should leave with. His brother, who came across like an obnoxious and antagonistic jerk, or the stranger dressed as a woman.

"Kenny," said Fuchsia in a stern tone reminiscent of his mother's, "you think about our conversation back there. If you want to do what you *said* you wanted to do, then come with me."

"Bro, come on. You can't be serious. Let's go."

"Whatever you do, Kenny, it will change your life," said Fuchsia in a low tone, so that only Kenny could hear.

He decided. "Chet, thanks for getting me out. Fuchsia? Let's go."

He ignored his brother's protestations, which he peppered with derisiveness and punctuated with guffaws. Fuchsia walked out ahead of Kenny as if the corridor was a catwalk, and though he didn't exactly follow suit, he kept his head high and his back straight. Though his body was unaccustomed—uncomfortable even—in the stance, it further strengthened his resolve. One new Kenny, coming up.

⁹ LEE

Lee stopped into the first tourist shop she saw on Gulf Boulevard and bought an outfit the Old Lee would rather be caught dead in than wear in public. The Cher outfit had served its purpose, but now she needed something beach-town appropriate.

Lee scoured each rack for just the right thing. Flowy, thin dresses, micro-short shorts, barely-there tops. Then she saw it. A pair of silky, teal harem-style pants and a matching crop top. She still had the body to pull it off. That's what the salesgirl said, at least. Lee didn't appreciate the *still*, but she accepted the compliment.

"Can I wear it out of the store?"

The girl snapped her gum and said, "Whatever floats your boat, ma'am."

From there, she spied a tattoo shop across the street. Ten minutes later, she found herself in a black, dentist style chair, staring up into the forget-me-not blue eyes of a man who called himself Phoenix as he explained the process.

"So, you pick out your tattoo, I'll sketch it up. Pick your placement, give it a trial run, then make the magic happen. You know what you want?"

Lee looked around at the dozens of framed drawings for inspiration. None of them called to her. Phoenix crossed his heavily tattooed arms over his chest and waited. She tried to be unfazed by his piercing gaze.

After several minutes went by, he suggested, "Most people pick something symbolic for their first tat. Unless they're drunk."

"I-oh, no. I'm sober," assured Lee. "Something symbolic, hmm?"

She thought hard. What could she choose that would *mean* something?"

Phoenix chuckled. "Don't *over*think it. Clear your mind, let your body relax. Imagine yourself as a bird, flying. Light. Free, Open to—"

Lee sat up straight, her eyes bright. "That's it. That's what I want, a bird." Phoenix smiled, and Lee understood he'd supplanted the idea, but she didn't mind. She smiled back. "You've been doing this for a while, haven't you?"

Phoenix shrugged. "Only about twenty years. Sometimes I know right away what someone needs. Soon as *you* walked in, I saw it."

"Oh, yeah? And what kind of bird do you see when you look at me?"

Flirting? Lee Harper, *flirting*. She hoped he'd say hummingbird or maybe a cardinal, and feared he'd say a wren or starling. The boring birds. He surprised her.

"Goldfinch."

"Goldfinch?" She thought about it a moment, then grinned. "Yeah, goldfinch. I like that."

"Great. Now, where do you want it?"

Again, Lee pondered. If she put it on her shoulder—her first pick—then she'd never see it without a mirror. On her bicep seemed to manly. Her bikini line? Ankle?

"Hip," said Phoenix.

He touched her waist just above the line of her new, ultra-low riding pants. His finger felt warm, but it sent a shiver throughout Lee's body. With a shock, Lee realized she *wanted* to be touched. How long had it been since she desired a man's hands on her? Too long.

"Y-yes. Hip."

Phoenix winked and promised to be back quickly. When he returned, he had the sketch on a filmy white square of paper. "You ready?"

"As I'll ever be," said Lee.

He reclined the chair until flat, checked her comfort level, and walked her through each step.

"Okay, first, I'm gonna stick this guy on here—just gotta lower your pants a bit more—and peel off the paper, and now here's a mirror." He gave her a hand-held mirror, "What do you think? Stand up, if you want, and look in the full length."

She did. The purple outline rested in the hollow beside her hip bone, barely above her panty line. She loved it.

"It's perfect, Phoenix."

"Great. Hop back up there, little birdy, and let's get started."

Two hours and a half later, Lee walked out into the sunlight with three hundred dollars less in her pocket, a little bit sore, but a thousand times lighter than she'd ever felt. She pulled her brand-new sunglasses off her head and shook her hair out. Next stop, a cocktail.

"Cappy's, here I come."

She followed her phone's navigation, tracking her progress. Seven minutes away.

"Whoa, watch your step, sweetheart."

A strong hand gripped her arm and she jerked her head up to gaze into yet another pair of blue eyes, these with flecks of green.

"What? I—"

"Walking into oncoming traffic won't get you where you trying to go, lady."

He nodded at the 'don't walk' light. She glanced at it, then at the ragged line of approaching cars. They weren't traveling very fast, and she technically had time to cross, if she sprinted. Lee didn't want to sprint, nor did she want to wait. What would hippie woman do if a gorgeous man had just rescued her? Surely, she wouldn't simper and swoon. She'd tease and flirt with the man. So, Lee slipped out of his grasp and crossed at a leisurely pace, giving her hips an extra sway. It scratched at her new tattoo, but she ignored the pain.

Over her shoulder, she called back, "Thanks, big guy. Don't worry, they'll stop."

A second later he clamped her elbow again, this time pulling her along to the opposite side. A few horns honked. Lee giggled, exhilarated.

"Well, that was fun."

"Lady, are you drunk, or high, or something? I know this isn't New York City, but still. You can't—"

"Nick! Nick Keller, you *asshole*," yelled a leggy blonde in an orange string bikini.

The man, still holding Lee's elbow, muttered, "Shit."

The Amazonian blonde—looking like something out of the Sports Illustrated Swimsuit magazine—stormed over to them, slit her eyes at Lee, and glared at the man who was apparently Nick.

"What the hell, Nick? You said you were going to Cappy's to grab more drinks over an hour ago. Now here you are with this... this slut?"

"Whoa, whoa. Jesus, Keely, calm down. I was just—"

"Excuse me? Did you just call me a slut? *Me*? A *slut*?"

The towering, model woman placed her hands on her hips and thrust her chin at Lee. "That's right. I did."

Lee smiled and laughed. "That's… that's wonderful. No one's ever called me a-a slut before. Thank you. I mean it, really. Thank you. Well, bye now."

Lee strolled away from the pair still giggling. Lee Harper had been called a prude, a stick-in-the-mud, a plain Jane, and even a Stepford Wife—that one from Kenny's idiot brother, Chet—but no one had ever mistaken her for a loose woman of questionable morals. How very exciting.

At last, she reached the sand swept step of Cappy's. The sounds of Jimmy Buffet's Margaritaville spilled out as she stepped in. High tables and bar stools, a Tiki-style bar complete with thatched roof, and a small stage took up the front half of the restaurant, which opened to picnic tables in the sand under an awning.

Further in, separated only by a half-wall, were regular tables, restrooms, and the kitchen. A waitress in tight black shorts and a tank top told her to sit wherever she'd like. It was a weekday and off-season and there were several available tables to choose from, excluding one in the corner with a group of three—a man and two women—who obviously had been drinking for a while. Lee picked a high table that offered the best view of both the beach and the musician on the stage, and far from the drunken trio.

"What can I get you, honey," asked the waitress.

The man onstage continued singing Margaritaville.

"I'll have a margarita, please." She'd never had one before.

"Sure thing. Traditional, strawberry, mango, or raspberry?

"Oh. I think... mango."

"Something to eat? Our seafood chowder is popular."

Old Lee would never order something so heavy. Especially from a place with sand on the floors. "Perfect, I'll have that."

A few minutes later, her frozen, mango-colored, sugar-rimmed, and pink umbrella'd drink sat before her. Lee took a small sip through the paper straw. Amazing. She took another, bigger sip, and an excruciating pain stabbed the back of her eyes and temples.

"Place your tongue on the roof of your mouth. It stops the brain freeze."

Lee did so and felt immediate relief. She twisted in her seat to see the musician beside her, smiling. Lee smiled back, thanked him, and took another sip. He sat down beside her.

"You're welcome. I don't think I've seen you around before. I'm Max."

"Hi, Max. I'm Lee. And no, I've never been here before."

"New in town? Or just visiting?"

"Oh, I've lived in the area—Dunedin, specifically—for almost twenty years. We—I moved here from Connecticut. I've just never been here, specifically."

"So, what brings you here—specifically—today?"

Lee studied Max and considered how much to tell him. She put him in his forties, based on the lines etched into the corners of his eyes and mouth when he smiled, and the silver hairs woven into the black at his temples. He wore it long-ish and tousled, something could never picture Kenny doing. Max also wore a small, gold hoop earring in his ear and a simple gold chain around his neck with a music note pendant. Kenny wore no jewelry aside from his wedding band. Comparing the two men could only mean one thing. She felt attracted to the beach bar musician. Lee blushed.

"Sorry, was that intrusive? You don't have to answer," said Max.

"Oh, no, not at all," Lee hurried to reassure him and moved to put a hand on his arm.

The move proved to too quick for an unevenly balanced bar stool, and Lee slipped toward Max. In one fluid motion, he sprang to his feet, grabbed hold of her elbow in one hand and her hip in the other, and slid her back onto her seat.

"Thank—"

The next word caught in her throat because the incredibly cute, crinkly-eyed man now stood a breath away, standing in between her legs most intimately. His hand, strong and warm, remained on her hip. She glanced down at it, as did he.

"Sorry," said Max. He removed his hands with a sheepish grin.

She tried to hide her disappointment when he took his hands off her waist and stepped out from between her legs. He didn't return to his seat, however, and instead stood close to her. This pleased her more than she could believe possible. She felt like a giddy teenage girl with a crush.

"No, no. You're fine. It's fine, I mean." Lee blushed again.

"Well, any time you want to fall into my arms is fine by me, Lee."

Her name from his lips, his hands on her skin, those eyes...

"Paul McCartney," she sighed.

Max blinked, then laughed. "I—did you just say Paul McCartney?"

She nodded once. "That's who you remind me of. I couldn't think of it until just now."

He smiled again and Lee almost swooned with lust. "I've heard that a time or two before, I admit. Are you a McCartney fan?" He put his hands together in prayer. "Please say yes. I, um, do a not-so-bad tribute set."

She answered him honestly. "I love Paul McCartney."

Lee blushed again. It was like saying to Max that she loved *him*. How mortifying. But Max rewarded her with a euphoric shout of joy, even raising his fists to the sky.

"Yes, thank you Lord for sending me the most beautiful woman in the state, *and* having her love my favorite Beatle."

Lee giggled and practically swooned again. *Beautiful*. He called her beautiful. *Oh, what fun*. The chatted about music for a few more minutes and Max ordered her another margarita and one for himself.

"Shit, break's over. Say you'll stay for a while?"

"Yes, Max, I'll stay," said Lee, her grin now a permanent fixture.

Like Lee, Max's expression and behavior recalled that of a teenager. He practically burst with exuberance. More thrilling, though, was the look in his eyes as he gazed at Lee. She couldn't name it, that look. It had never been something she'd been on the receiving end of, but if she had to guess, they word might be adoration.

"Crystal," he called to the waitress, "anything the lady wants is on me."

Crystal's eyebrows shot up and she looked back and forth between Max and Lee. "Uh, sure thing, Max."

The noisy threesome in the corner took notice, too. They all exchanged glances that Lee recognized as amazement. Obviously, they all knew Max, and his attention to Lee surprised them. Then it dawned on her. *He's married. That's* why they're exchanging those looks. She deflated a little, then became defensive. *Harmless flirtation. Nothing would happen. Technically, she was married, too.*

Max had returned to the stage and Lee sucked down half her drink, using his trick to combat the brain freeze. Lee felt darn—no, *damn* good. Better than she'd ever felt in her whole life, come to think of it. She swayed as he sang a song about a girl named Brandy and stood to dance when he played a fun Neil Diamond song.

When that song ended, he strummed a few chords on his guitar, his head down. Into the microphone, he said, "All right, now, folks, I'd like to sing couple songs for a special lady."

He tilted his head and gave Lee a side glance and slow smile. Lee's expression matched his and she put her hand to her heart. No one had ever dedicated a song to her.

"Lee, sweetheart, do you have a favorite?"

Without hesitation, Lee said, "Don't Let Me Down."

Max looked at her as if she'd just handed him a billion-dollar winning lottery ticket. The corner trio had all but ceased their raucous banter and now watched Lee and Max with keen interest.

Into the microphone he said, "Do you sing, Lee?"

He smiled at her, but his eyes were serious. Lee half-shrugged and looked away. She'd sung all her life, but only as part of a chorus in school and in her church choir. Always the back row. Never center stage.

New life, new Lee.

She filled her lungs and straightened her spine and met his steady gaze. Almost imperceptivity, she bobbed her head, once. He saw it.

"Jimmy, grab another stool for me, will you?"

"You got it, man."

The beefy young man behind the Tiki bar sprang around the counter, grabbed a seat at the end, and ran it up to Max. The stage stood elevated only a foot, but Jimmy the bartender handed her up like a gentleman. Like a *princess*. She could get used to this.

"I'll start, you jump in when you feel comfortable, okay?"

"Okay," said Lee. Her voice shook.

Lee focused only on Max and tried not to think about all the eyes on them. The first line of the chorus sounded shaky, too soft. He pressed his knee against hers and nodded as they sang. By the second chorus her voice rang clear underneath his. By the third, it equaled it. The song ended and the room erupted in applause.

Max gestured to her and said, "Please give a special hand to Lee..." He trailed off, not knowing her last name, but recovered quickly, "the lovely Lee."

Louder applause commenced. Lee, startled, looked around at all the new faces. People had come in off the beach to listen. She pressed her hands to her hot cheeks and exhaled, her eyes sparkling with unshed happy tears.

"What do you say? Should she sing another song?"

Cheers and a few shouts of 'hell, yes' greeted them.

"Oh, Max, I don't—"

"Your fans want more, sweetheart. Don't let them down." He winked.

Lee laughed and rolled her eyes at him. If Lee had ever had wildest dreams, this surpassed them.

She held up a finger and said, "One more."

Max leaned over, kissed her cheek, and whispered, "That a girl. You got this."

One more song turned into three, finishing out Max's last set for the day. He sent her to see Jimmy at the Tiki bar while he packed up his gear.

"I'm just going to toss this stuff in the car. Be right back." He walked away, then turned back, a look of concern clouding his face. "You'll stay, right? You won't leave?"

Lee's heart swelled. "I'll be right here when you get back, Max. I promise."

Jimmy brought her another drink — her third — and told her she did a great job.

"Really? You're not just saying that, are you?"

"Hell, no. Besides, Max would never bring anyone up onstage he didn't think could sing."

A voice beside her said, "Max has never given any woman more than the time of day, honey. Hi, I'm Margot. This is Lucy, and the guy flirting with the Ricky Martin look-a-like over there is Carlos."

"Charmed," said Lucy.

"Hello. I'm Lee. You, uh, you're all friends with Max?"

The woman named Margot nodded and leaned in like a spy expecting the secret code word. "All right, toots. What's your superpower? Chicks have been trying to turn his head forever."

"Oh, I—"

Lucy piped in. "You know he lost his wife a couple years ago, right?"

"No, I—"

"So tragic. The Big C."

Lee's heart clenched. Poor Max. Did it make her a terrible person to feel a little relieved, too? And flattered.

"So, who's our sexy little mystery lady?" Carlos joined them, stuffing what might have been a slip of paper with a phone number into his shorts pocket.

Before she could answer, Lucy said, "Her name is Lee and her outfit is bangin'"

Margot scoffed. "You're too old to say bangin', Lucy."

"*You're* too old to wear those shorts, but I'm not judging," retorted Lucy.

Dismayed, Lee jumped in. "Stop, you're both perfect, and gorgeous. Who the hell has the right to tell us what we can and can't wear, or say, or feel? Just because we're not in our twenties anymore?"

"You know what?" Margot slammed down her drink. "You're abso-fucking-lutely right, Lee. Fuck them, whoever they are."

'Yeah," said Carlos, appeared to not know what was going on, but not caring, either. "Fuck them, fuck me, fuck it all."

He lifted his margarita high and saluted the rest of the patrons, all twenty or so at the bar. Everyone raised their drinks and a chorus of, 'Fuck it all' rang out. Lee joined in with as much gusto as the rest. She turned to see Max smiling at her from the entrance. He waved her over and she excused herself from the roaringly drunk trio.

"Would you like to take a walk on the beach with me? The sun will set soon, and — I know it'll sound cliché — but there's nothing more beautiful than a beach sunset, don't you think?"

"I do," said Lee.

She took his outstretched hand and they left the bar. At the row of beach chairs outside Cappy's, they kicked off their shoes before strolling along the shore. The sun, now a deep orange globe, had sunk lower in the sky toward the watery horizon, and Lee felt certain she'd seen nothing so beautiful.

She and Kenny visited the beach often since they moved to Florida, but it was always a very concise, organized production. Two chairs, one cooler, SPF 50 for Kenny and SPF 24 for Lee. Arrival: precisely at ten AM. Eat lunch at twelve. Take one walk along the beach at twelve-forty-five. Pack up and leave at two PM. They brought books to read and papers to grade.

"I suppose this is pretty cliché for a woman like you, right?"

"What makes you say that?"

"Well, you're beautiful, so I'm sure plenty of men have tried to make grand romantic gestures to impress you."

"Are *you* trying to impress me, Max?"

If she didn't know better, she'd say that Max blushed. She recalled Margot's words about his wife dying.

In a gentler tone, she said, "I *am* impressed, Max. This has been the best afternoon of my whole life."

Now she blushed. Max stopped and pulled her close, his gaze solemn and earnest. The gentle breeze had blown her hair around, and he brushed the errant strands behind her ear. He didn't take his hand away but cupped her face.

"I'd like to kiss you," said Max, a tremor in his voice.

Lee tilted her face to his and for the first time in nearly twenty years, she kissed with passion and abandon. He pulled back just enough to rest his forehead against hers and caress her cheek. Her arms were around his back, gripping his shirt. He placed a light, tender kiss on her lips, and said in a hushed voice, "Turn around."

He turned her by her shoulders to see the most spectacular sunset she'd ever witnessed. The sky looked like a painter's canvas, streaked in a riot of purple, red, blue and orange. The persimmon sun touched the water and lit it aflame. Water on fire. She knew of course, didn't really touch the water, but for once in her life, Lee allowed herself to imagine. She stepped back into Max's arms with a sigh. They stayed that way until all that remained of the sun was a warm halo.

"We can walk a little further, down to the pier, if you'd like. Or..." he hesitated, "we could walk in the other direction. Where my bungalow is."

He seemed to be holding his breath. She knew she did. Yet Max's nervousness emboldened her. She wanted this, *him*. Maybe the alcohol or maybe the sunset made her do it, but Lee took his hand and pulled them in the opposite direction of the pier.

¹⁰ TEN

Since the pre-dawn hour woke her with a heavy weight on her chest—initially inexplicable until she recalled the sickening news of her brain tumor—Ten expected the sunrise to bring with it more of that flooring sense of reality and impending doom, but no.

She rose at seven, blended her special concoction of coffee, cinnamon, turmeric, and almond milk, poured it over ice in her travel cup, and began her day. Same as she always had.

I'm fine, everything is fine, I'm fine. The mantra had morphed into a song.

While one part of her brain anticipated the big melt-down that *had* to be coming any moment now, the other said 'just keep swimming' in that cartoon fish voice. In Ten's case, just keep swimming meant collect her client's dogs and start their daily walk. So, that's what she did.

At eight on the dot, Ten, Fitz and Lizzy let the Schnauzers—Leopold and Luanne—lead the pack of seven dogs and one human. Most days Augustus, the German shepherd, set the pace but he was home recovering from a minor surgery. All but Francine, the Yorkshire terrier, were well-behaved and walked with dignified indifference to the stares and outstretched hands of passersby.

"Cool it, Francine. You're making us look bad."

Francine yipped twice more, then glared up at Ten as if *she* were the absolute worst, and not the other way around. *Terriers. Always the terriers.* In her vast dog walking experience, the bigger the dog, the better behaved they were. Case in point, Max's Great Dane, Jude — litter mate of her beloved Fitz — was by far the best mannered dog she'd ever walked. But Mrs. Van Stephen had practically begged her to take Francine, and she couldn't refuse.

"I'll pay you double, Ten. Just take this little terrorist for a walk, please."

Ten donated all the money she made from dog-walking to the local animal shelter, a fact few of her clients knew. She'd laughed, "No need to pay double, Mrs. Van Stephen. I'll take her. The others will be a good influence, I'm sure."

They weren't. Francine remained a terrorist while the others remained unperturbed by her insolence. Ten, too, couldn't give more than a moment's irritation to the yapping furball. The sun shone on a brand-new day, the air smelled of salty sea, begonias and jasmine, and she was still alive and feeling fine. Definitely *not* the way she thought someone with a—*don't think the words*—should feel.

She passed by the little shops and smiled at the store owners who waved. All the while, her mind wrestled with her new reality.

I'm probably supposed to suddenly understand the meaning of life at a time like this.

But damned if she knew. Should she have canceled all her clients today? Should she be skydiving, or bungee jumping? If so, she was failing the dying game because she was the same Ten, doing the same things she always did. The phrase *get your affairs in order* came to mind. Get her affairs in order? Ten laughed out loud. When had Tenley Harper ever done anything with order?

Maybe God or the universe or whoever was trying to send her a message.

"Oh, you sent me a message all right," muttered Ten to the sky.

"Ten! Hey, Ten! There you are. I've been trying to get ahold of you since yesterday morning. Where have you been? Why haven't you answered any of my calls or texts?"

Shit. Josh.

She vowed last night to herself that she would talk to him, cut him loose like Kablooey said. Now here he stood, and she had nothing prepared. *Think, Harper, think.*

"Hey, Josh. I was going to call you after I finished walking the dogs. Sorry, I've been super busy."

"Oh, okay. Thought for a minute you were maybe blowing me off." He looked her up and down. "That's quite an outfit you got going on today, Ten."

Ten look down. She wore black combat boots, a patchwork peasant skirt, her favorite Kelly-green bikini top she crocheted herself, and a lime green vest. On her head she wore a black, wide-brimmed sun hat, and black sunglasses shielded her eyes.

She shrugged. "No different than anything I usually wear."

"Sure, I guess not, but... I don't know, I guess it's just a little more extra than usual. Not that I see anything wrong with it, you look hot as ever. Like really, really hot. So, listen I got some clients lined up at the gym, but after you want to grab some lunch at Cappy's?"

Ten's first instinct was to make an excuse. Then she realized this could be part of *getting her affairs in order*, so she agreed. He leaned in to kiss her, and she gave him her cheek. He looks surprised and hurt, and a twinge of guilt flitted through her.

Josh jogged on ahead, affording Ten a lingering view of why she'd kept him around for as long as she did. He really was a sweetheart. A shame it had to end so soon. A shame everything had to end so soon.

Ah, here comes the melt-down. The big fall-apart. The reality.

Nope. Nothing. Maybe the brain tumor squished some neurotransmitter in her head and rendering it impossible for her to feel. Yes, that had to be it. Or, the power of denial was really that strong.

Another voice cut through the morning air—and Ten's quasi-peaceful, seven-dog walk—interrupting her ruminations.

"Ten! Tenley! Wait the fuck up. Jesus."

Margot huffed and puffed and walk-ran toward Ten.

"Hey momma, what are you doing up and out this early?"

"Shut up, I get up before eleven... most days. Okay fine *occasionally* I get up before eleven. The spa doesn't open until noon, so, whatever. I love that fucking hat, by the way."

Margot Mackie—Ten's friend of about five years— was forty-nine, ginger-haired, hourglass curved, occasionally reliable, and often vulgar. They'd met when Margot dated Ten's father for a few months. Margot sought husband number three, Charlie wanted a good time. Ten got stuck being the breaker-upper. When their 'nice knowing you while it lasted' drink turned into several more, it developed into a friendship. Turned out Margot wasn't as bad an opportunist as Ten suspected her to be and genuinely like her father, an endearing sentiment.

Though still in search of husband number three, Margot seemed content with her life. She shared a condo with Carlos and Lucy, worked four days a week in the spa as a massage therapist, one night a week bartending, and spent most of her free time on the beach or in Cappy's. Ten's father, in citing why he wasn't interested in furthering their relationship, said she was unambitious and complacent. Ten had argued she was merely content. Now, she supposed it would've been weird to have Margot as her stepmother. But then, it wouldn't have been so terrible either. Ultimately, Ten felt relieved on Margot's behalf that she'd be spared playing nurse to an eventual invalid and a dying step-daughter.

"Here. All yours."

Ten plucked the hat off her head and dropped it onto Margot's.

"Shit, really? Thanks. Hey, what's going on with you, kid? You weren't acting right yesterday, and a little birdy told me *Nick Keller* walked you home. Nick fucking Keller? Say it isn't so."

"A little birdy, huh? Who would that be? Never mind, it doesn't matter. And he didn't walk me home. More like followed me."

Margot squinted at Ten. "You still got a thing for him?"

The dogs pulled. "I never—listen, I'd love to chat, but these guys will lose it if I don't keep moving. Welcome to walk with—"

"Oh, God, no. Still hung over from yesterday. Oh, my God, that reminds me. Guess who left Cappy's with a woman last night?"

"Carlos?" They both burst out laughing. "Okay, okay, I give. Hurry and tell me before they yank my arm off."

"*Max*. Our Mr. Lonely Hearts Max Rivers left with a woman. Can you believe it?"

"Holy shit," said Ten with genuine surprise.

Everyone at the bar knew poor Max's story. Women had been trying almost since the day he buried his wife to be the next in line, but he'd never shown an ounce of interest. Even she could admit to a small crush on the guy. Ten's curiosity piqued.

"Yes, a real looker, too. Meet me at Cappy's later and I'll tell you all about her. Hell, maybe she'll even be there, and you can see for yourself."

The last part Margot had to yell since the dogs had finally won and pulled Ten down the street.

"Okay, sounds like a plan," called Ten over her shoulder.

She felt like she forgot something, another thing she was supposed to do. Ten shrugged. She'd figure it out later. For the time being, she needed to focus on what the hell to do for the rest of her life. All six to ten months of it. Bungee jumping sounded a little less ridiculous by the minute.

<u>11</u> <u>LEE</u>

Lee woke up in the arms of the best lover she'd even known. Granted, there'd only been two before him, but still. Her head rested on his smooth, bare chest and their toes peeked out of the tangled sheets. She'd slept naked, another first.

"Good morning," said Max.

He turned on his side to face Lee, one arm tucked under his head and the other wrapped around her. His chin and cheeks were stubbled black and silver and when he smiled—a slow, sleepy, and very sexy smile—a dimple appeared. Lee felt her body respond.

"Good morning."

Lee stretched against the length of him, hooking her leg over his waist and pulled his pelvis toward hers. He needed no further encouragement. Max cupped her backside and thrust inside her. She gripped his hair and primal sounds of ecstasy escaped her lips. When it ended, they fell back onto the sheets.

"Who the hell are you, Lee? Where'd you come from," panted Max. He tilted his head to look at her. "And how do I convince you to stay?"

Lee knew everything about this screamed crazy, and yet she didn't care. She was tired of following all the rules, all the time. So, what if they didn't know each other from a hole in the wall? Who cares if it moved at warp speed? Though she'd been given an extended stay, she knew life was short and she planned on making the most of it.

She giggled. "My name is Lee Merriweather, I'm thirty-six, I am — I *was* a fifth grade English teacher, and I am in bed with the sweetest, sexiest man I've ever met in my life. So, yes, Max, I'll stay. For now, at least."

She didn't say Merriweather was her maiden name. Or that technically she was still married. Seeing she hadn't worn her wedding ring years; she had no real need to elaborate. As for the rest, she figure it out as she went.

"I'll take it," grinned Max. "You hungry?"

"Ravenous."

Lee, who'd only eaten grapefruit and toast for breakfast for the past ten years, suddenly wanted eggs and bacon, pancakes, home fries, and a pot of coffee.

"Me, too. You're welcome to raid my drawers for some fresh clothes till we get your stuff. I'll run over to Cappy's, get my car, and we'll go into town for some grub."

From the bed, Lee watched him pull on a pair of shorts, a t-shirt, and rake his hair back. Where Kenny's body was full of points and sharp angles that often jabbed and poked Lee, Max was built solid, almost square.

She especially liked his forearms, which were sinewy and taut from years of playing guitar. Lee recalled them on either side of her head as they made love the night before. The stirrings of lust almost made her call him back to bed, but the rumble in her stomach silenced her.

When he left, she took a quick shower, noticing at once that his bathroom was clean, tidy, and smelled only of men's scents. No women's razors or second toothbrushes, no companion towel hanging from the hooks behind the door.

While wrapped in his towel—she'd *never* used Kenny's towel—Lee dug through Max's drawers for something to wear. She held one of his black tank tops against her. It would fit her like a short dress. Perfect. A tie scavenged from his closet served as a belt. She studied herself in the long mirror behind his bedroom door.

"Well look at you, Lee Harper. Who would have guessed?"

The living room was open, airy, and divided into a music and a sitting area. The musician side homed a well-loved black piano, a rack of guitars, several amps, a music stand, stool, microphone, and side table with sheets of music and a notepad. This left just enough room for a love seat, chair, coffee table, and a bookcase framing his tv on the opposite side of the room. Lee gravitated toward the line of pictures on top of the piano.

A couple black and white photos of what were likely Max's parents, others from childhood, a few of Max posing in his police uniform with fellow officers. Lee initially thought he'd been joking when he said he was a retired sergeant from New York, but here was further proof. In Lee's estimation, he made just as handsome an officer as he did a musician.

She steeled herself for the next set of photographs, all of which featured a stunning brunette with a full, wide smile and pale blue eyes. A coy smile at the camera in one. A profile shot of her staring out over the sea. Her slung over Max's shoulder, caught laughing. Them kissing. Five more, all different, all showing one singular focus.

The last picture was a wedding photo. They gazed into each other's eyes, slices of wedding cake in their hands poised to feed each other. She picked it up and studied it more. She was captivating, his wife. No question about it. It didn't take much imagining beyond those pictures to know Max and his wife's love story ended too soon and would likely still be going strong today had they the chance. Then again, what did she know?

She realized she knew *nothing* of this man. He had yet to speak of his dead wife and she only knew of her because of the crazy threesome at Cappy's. Lee checked herself. *You're having an adventure. Nothing more. Don't get attached to the first man you sleep with, silly.* Lee set the frame back on the piano, careful to place right tenley where she found it.

The one-bedroom bungalow had an open floor plan, so her exploration came to a quick end. An island separated the living room and kitchen, and there didn't seem to be much to see there, so Lee went back into the bedroom and climbed in bed. The closest Lee had ever come to lounging around had been when she had the flu, and that happened over a year ago.

This—slipping between an unfamiliar man's cool sheets, wearing his clothes and smelling of his shampoo—felt decadent and delicious. Lee stretched cat-like then curled around Max's pillow, smiling against the cotton. From the other side of the house came the sound of the door opening, then an unfamiliar, female voice called out.

"Yo, Maxie. Jude was a good boy as usual. Fitz and Lizzy loved their playdate. Text me if you want me to take him again next week. Gotta run."

Lee bolted upright as the door slammed shut. A sound that her brain couldn't immediately process followed. By the time she understood, a gigantic, heavy-breathing, massive-snouted dog stood on top of her in the bed.

She'd barely gotten the covers up to her chin before the mammoth beast licked her face with his ping-pong paddle-sized tongue.

"Stop," she said in between face-soaking tongue slaps. "Get off. Go on, now."

The horse-dog stopped, tilted his head, whined once, and laid down partly on top of Lee, partly on the bed, trapping her beneath him. He stared expectantly at her.

"Okay. All right. This is... different."

She reached a tentative hand out from underneath the covers and patted his knobby head. Unlike Dexter's silkiness, but still soft. Lee had always liked dogs in theory but had little experience with them. Her father had been allergic, as had Kenny. So, there went any hope of ever being a dog owner.

Where Dexter seemed indifferent and unimpressed by Lee's attempts to communicate with him, this creature seemed to be waiting and even hoping for more. So, feeling silly, she obliged.

"Hey, Jude." She giggled. "Bet you've never heard that before."

The Great Dane whined, then nosed her hand back onto his head.

"Oh, you're just a big baby, aren't you?"

Lee stroked his soft pate and the giant inched closer.

"Well, I see you two are fast friends," laughed Max from the doorway. "Jude, you traitor."

Max climbed onto the bed, two coffees in hand. Jude switched allegiances and rolled over to his person, nearly knocking the coffees from his hands.

"Whoa, easy buddy," laughed Max, unperturbed.

Lee's heart near-burst with an emotion that felt suspiciously like love. Ever pragmatic, her instinct was to shove the irrational feeling down into the well where impractical thoughts lived. But the old Lee did that. What would new Lee do?

Max, who'd been forehead to sloped forehead with Jude and talking in that funny way dog owners speak to their pets, lifted his eyes to hers. Their gazes locked and unsaid words passed between them.

What is this?

I'm not sure.

Can it last?

Will you stay?

I might love you.

I know I love you.

Stay.

I will.

"Hello, you."

"Hello, you. What shall we do today?"

Lee needed not to reply, her stomach grumbled her answer.

Max laughed. "There's a café in walking distance. You ready?"

Lee hopped out of bed, danced a quick twirl, and sang, "Ta-da."

Max whistled slow and low. "Hello, lovely. My shirt has never looked so good."

"Don't get any ideas, mister. I'm starving. Feed me, then maybe..." She waggled her eyebrows.

"Say no more, my love." Max sprang from the bed, Jude in tow. "Sorry, buddy, you've already had your walk."

"Oh, that reminds me, your dog walker said Jude had a great playdate with Fritz and Libby, and to text her if you want her to take him next week. Or something like that."

Max chuckled. "Fitz and Lizzy. Did you get to meet the rest of the dogs?"

"Oh, no. I was in bed when she let Jude in. Is she... a friend of yours?"

Lee tried to sound nonchalant and failed, based on Max's amused expression.

"Yes, she is. Just a friend, though. Always has been, always will be. Jude and her Fitz are litter mates, as a matter of fact."

Lee didn't know why she'd felt such a silly rush of jealousy over a woman she only heard but not seen. Her irrational side thought the woman *sounded* pretty. Vaguely familiar even. She dismissed the idea, and her pettiness, too.

"I'm ready if you are," said Lee with a grin.

<u>12</u> <u>MAX</u>

Max had hurried to Cappy's parking lot. There was a beautiful, sexy, and mysterious woman in his bed, and he wanted to get back there as fast as possible. The sun shone down on a new day. Everything in his universe neared perfect. So, when a sudden melancholy wormed its way into his thoughts, it confused him. Then, as it always did, understanding came.

Elena. Sweet, funny Elena, his wife of only five years. Gone from him and this earth for three years. This was how it happened now. Long stretches of fine, then the sudden stab of remembering. The knife—now dulled by time—used to be sharp, serrated and relentlessly painful.

The first six months after Elena died, he couldn't sleep, couldn't stop seeing her face everywhere and in everything. It was six months of darkness and despair.

He hoarded the memories like they were treasures. They *were* treasures. Max holed himself in their little house by the sea and wrapped her ghost around himself. He slept all day, stayed awake all night. He allowed no one in and he never went out. Ten and the others—who were more acquaintances from Cappy's than friends in the beginning—brought food and offers of companionship. He turned them all away.

All he wanted was for the scent of her on his pillows to remain, her clothes to stay in the closet. He left her toothbrush by the sink. On day, he spied her hairbrush on her dresser, her long chestnut hair wound into the bristles. He held it in his hand for so long and tightly, his fingers cramped.

Photographs, videos, and audio recordings of her trying to sing along with him played non-stop. Day in and day out. Her voice filled every inch of their home. She had a terrible singing voice, and he loved it. Loved her only imperfection. To him, she was otherwise flawless. His ethereal angel made mortal, then stolen back again.

When the suffocating grief became more than he could bear, he let anger enter his pores. He welcomed it. He raged against an unfair God, the doctors who couldn't cure her, and lastly... Elena. Why, *why* had she not gone to the doctor sooner?

She knew her family history—her grandmother, mother, and two sisters, all with breast cancer—and yet she put off making an appointment until it was too late.

In one of those fits, he knocked all the photographs into the trash along with their wedding album, her clothes, everything he could find that bore traces of Elena. The next day the trash collectors came. The horror at what he'd done suffused him at the sound of the hydraulic hiss and thud of the barrel being set back down. Max ran out in his shorts and stained shirt, his hair wild. He chased the truck to the next stop and begged them to let him retrieve his bags.

They thought he was a madman. They were right. Ten passed by with her dogs, and upon seeing Max and the commotion, stopped.

"Maxie, babe. What's going on?"

One man said, "This guy is crazy, lady. He wants his trash back. I'm trying to tell him—"

"Hang on, okay? Please?"

"Max, why do you want your trash back?"

Max's stubbled chin trembled. "Ten, I-I threw her away. I threw her—"

Understanding flooded Ten's eyes. "I got you, Maxie. We'll get her back."

She left Max with her dogs and whispered to the two men. Max had no idea what she'd said to them, but minutes later the men opened the back of truck, and they could retrieve most of the discarded items. She walked back to the house with him, trash bags slung over their shoulders and Fitz and Lizzy in the lead. They said little and Ten kept her expression neutral when she stepped inside the shuttered, stale smelling house.

Max had sat down on the sofa, cradling the bag with Elena's clothes. Ten sent the dogs out into the backyard with Jude, and with a library-like quietness set his house back in order. She lined the piano with the photographs, set the wedding album on a bookcase shelf, cleared away the beer bottles and pizza boxes that littered the coffee table. Running water and the clank of dishes and silverware came from the kitchen. Max had stayed put, his arms around the damn trash bag, his gaze fixed on the cobalt blue vase on the table, the one that matched Elena's eyes.

After a while, Ten had sat down beside him, smelling of lemon cleaner and her bergamot and rose perfume. She rested her hand on his and dropped her head on his shoulder.

"Come back to us, Maxie. We miss you."

Had she said, 'Time to move on,' or 'Would Elena want you to live like this,' he might not have swayed. But in true Tenley Harper fashion, she knew the right thing to say to soften Max's heart.

His voice husky, he said, "Miss you guys, too. Thanks, Ten."

She patted his hand and stood. "I'll take Jude for a walk with Fitz and Lizzy. You do what you need to do and then tonight, I expect to see you with that black guitar of yours at Cappy's."

It wasn't a request. Max, for the first time in a while, grinned. "Yes, ma'am. Will do."

He waited twenty minutes longer after she'd gone with the dogs. Then, Max stood, set the bag aside, and went around the house raising the shades and cranking open windows. In the bathroom, he stripped off the dingy shirt and shorts and took a cool shower. He shaved, dressed, and slicked back his hair. When he met his gaze in the mirror, he didn't quite see the man he used to be, but it was close.

"It's time, old man."

With music playing through the built-in speakers, Max went systematically through the house and rid it of the shrine-like appearance. He filled boxes for donation and others for her sister's perusal. He saved sentimental mementos and discarded the rest. He rearranged the furniture and hung some of his old framed prints on the walls. The Beatles on one side, Elvis on the other.

By the end of the day, Max and Elena's house looked like Max's house. It surprised him to have stayed dry-eyed throughout, and the sudden weight of guilt forced him to sit down. It had only been eight months. How could he erase her in just mere hours?

Then her song came on—No Matter What—and Max laughed and cried at the same time.

Elena loved that song—the lyrics so happy and upbeat, so forever sounding—and Max couldn't help but love it, too.

No matter where you are, I will always be with you...

"Okay, Elena, my love. I hear you," said Max into the empty house.

That night he returned to Cappy's. He dedicated the first song to Elena. The second was to his friends, Ten, Margot, Lucy, Carlos and the rest of the hodge-podge crew assembled to welcome him back into the land of the living. It could be no other song than With A Little Help from My Friends. There were a lot of held-back tears that night.

Max got on with the business of life. He kept busy, played his music, met up with old friends from the PD who'd also retired in Florida, and stayed healthy. The one thing he didn't do—wouldn't do—was date. He wasn't trying to be a martyr, or some morose sad sack. He just wasn't interested.

Max had great love with his wife. The kind people dream of and wish for and write songs about, damn it. How could he settle for anything less than that? The answer was that he couldn't. It would be earth-shaking love, or none. After three years—years that flew by in an instant—Max resigned himself to the notion it might never happen again for him. Then Lee walked in.

He saw her the moment she came through the door. She looked like a little lioness. Then he caught the way her hand trembled as she tucked her hair behind her ear. He watched as she took a deep breath, straightened her spine, and strode across the room to a stool by the patio bar. She'd made eye contact with no one. Someone else might have seen arrogance in that purposeful stride. Not Max. He saw everything. Pride, determination, insecurity, bravery, grace. And yes, beauty. He couldn't take his eyes off her for more than a few seconds at a time.

The second his set ended he practically ran to her side. He'd been so afraid someone else would make a move on her first and he'd lose his chance. He been next to her a full minute before he could manage something to say. He cringed at the recollection. *Place your tongue to the roof of your mouth.*

Those were the first words he said to the woman he'd fallen instantly in love with? Why couldn't have been something more cool or suave? Still, she'd smiled at him and studied him with those wide hazel eyes and something primal in him awakened. He wanted her. Max wanted to touch her face and hold her against him, and when she slipped from her stool it was as if the universe had conspired to give him his wish.

It took all the restraint in the world not to kiss her then. When she spoke, he thought, '*I bet she can sing.*' She had that kind of voice, melodic even in speech. All too soon, he had to return to the stage. This time, when his eyes landed on her, she gazed back. Smiling.

Twenty-two years on the job had given him a good feel for people. He knew she was avoiding something, maybe even running. She wore no wedding ring, nor was there a tell-tale tan line—a ghost of a wedding ring newly shed. Not a husband. A boyfriend maybe? She didn't have the skittish kitten air of a battered woman, that much he was certain. Whatever it was, it seemed no worse than someone wanting a fresh start.

If anyone could understand that, it was Max Rivers. He'd loved his job, but by the end he was as done as a man could be. He'd seen more than most people could imagine—depravity and evil, psychotics and sociopaths, victims of every age and circumstance. It was the kids that got to him the most. He didn't like to think about it.

He'd met Elena in his last year on the job. They married and moved to Florida two months after he turned in his badge. She encouraged him to play his guitar again, something he'd given up several years back. It felt like putting on a favorite pair of slippers that fit just right. Still did.

In a way—a roundabout way—it was like Elena brought Lee to him. Had she not pushed him to play, then to offer his talent to Cappy's as a weekday acoustic musician, he wouldn't have been in there when she walked in. Maybe that was a stretch, but still. It felt nice to think of it that way, and it eased that low feeling in his chest.

As cliché as it was to say, Max knew Elena wanted him to find love again. She'd told him so. Made him swear on it, too. He hadn't told her he'd crossed his fingers behind his back when he made the promise, but she knew. She always knew what Max was thinking. A need to talk to her overwhelmed him.

Max detoured off the sidewalk and went down to the shoreline, where he could be alone. He wanted a minute to talk to his wife in the place he felt closest to her.

"Been a long time, Elena. Sorry about that. I just—" he took a deep breath, "I just want you to know, I'm keeping my promise, sweetheart. She's special. I, uh, I think you'd approve."

He looked down to see a pearl white shell and bent to pick it up. Elena had only collected white shells. Max chuckled, then pressed the shell to his lips before sending it back to the sea. He was ready to start the next chapter of his life.

[13] KENNY

Jacqui, with lightning fast hands and an even faster rate of speech washed, combed, and trimmed Kenny's hair with whisks and whispers of sharp steel blades. Mini tumbleweeds of his hair toppled over his caped shoulders onto the gleaming wood floor until at last she could only add small feathery wisps to the piles.

After a while, Jacqui stood behind him, and placed her hands on either side of his head, staring at his hair through the mirror like he was a canvas and she, an artist. Come to think of it, Kenny realized it was a form of art. *He* couldn't cut and sculpt his hair to look like anything. It impressed him, her skills. Thinking she might be finished; Kenny opened his mouth to thank her.

"Not done yet, sweetheart. You just sit pretty and let mama work her magic."

She stood thin sections of his hair up in between her fingers, stared hard at them, then whisk, whisk went the shears. Next, she squeezed out a dollop of clear liquid onto her palm, rubbed her hands together, and then ran her fingers through his hair every which way. Kenny tried hard not to stare at the line of cleavage and the café au lait swells under her tight blouse. He failed. Jacqui noticed, but instead of scowling, she winked and pinched his cheek.

"You ready to see the new you?"

Kenny blinked up at Jacqui, gulped, then nodded. She stepped aside, pulling the cape from his neck with a flourish. He looked in the oversized wall mirror at a man he almost didn't recognize. It was his reflection, he knew this, but... enhanced. Upgraded. Re-issued. And his head felt lighter, too.

"Well, look at you, Mr. GQ."

Fuchsia came up behind him, beside Jacqui. They high-fived each other, and Kenny, for the first time since his wife told him she wanted a divorce, smiled.

"I don't look like me, I look like—"

"Ryan Gosling's older brother," finished Jacqui.

Kenny still didn't know who Ryan Gosling was, but by the way Jacqui looked at him, he had an idea it might be a compliment. He could get used to this new version of Kenny Harper.

Fuchsia clapped in excitement. "All right, handsome. Time to get you into some modern threads, baby. You ready for round two?"

She looked from Kenny to Jacqui, then back again to Kenny.

"You know," Fuchsia intoned, "I'd love to go freshen up my own self. Maybe *you* could take Kenny shopping, Jacqui?"

Jacqui looked surprised, then pleased. At least, Kenny thought she looked pleased. He could've read it all wrong. He usually did. But when she agreed, even he could doubt it no more.

"I'd love to take him. Kenny, would you mind waiting for a few minutes while I clean up?"

Kenny knew he should've declined. He'd already delayed finding his wife and winning her back. So, the words that came out his mouth surprised him.

"Sure, I'll wait."

Twenty minutes later, Jacqui grabbed his hand and pulling him across the street, and not at the crosswalk.

"We could get a ticket for jaywalking, you know."

Jacqui glanced over her shoulder at him, rolled her eyes and laughed.

"Relax, Dudley-Do-Right. Besides, didn't you just get out of jail?"

"I—it was a misunder—"

"Hush, Dudley. I'm teasing." A minute later, she said, "You can let go of my hand now."

He looked down at their still clasped hands. Kenny loosened his grip but then almost, *almost* without thinking, curled his long fingers around her hand again. Jacqui gave him a smile he found hard to believe meant for him. He looked back to be sure a taller, better-looking man didn't stand behind him.

That's when he saw her. *Lee.* Or someone who looked very much like her, but in an outfit his wife would never wear in a million years. Instinct pulled him in the woman's direction who might be Lee.

"Uh, hello? Wrong way, the store we're going to is *this* way," said Jacqui.

"Oh, yeah, but I think I just—can we…"

Kenny trailed off, craning and bobbing his head to track the progress of the maybe-Lee woman. Alongside her, a dark-haired man with a guitar bag slung over his shoulder. He couldn't at first tell if they were together, too many people separated them. The man draped his arm over her slight shoulders proprietarily, leaving no further doubt in Kenny's mind. In a moment she—*they*—would be out of sight.

"Hey, slow down, will you? Running in heels is not fun," said Jacqui.

Kenny looked back at her, down at their hands. He'd forgotten her existence the moment he saw the Lee look-a-like.

"I'm really sorry, Jacqui, but I think my wife just went around that corner, and I—"

"Say no more."

She let go of his hand and put on a bright smile, but not before Kenny saw disappointment cloud her face. Kenny recognized *that* expression. He'd seen it on Lee's face more times than he'd like to remember. Seeing the look on Jacqui affected him with as much force.

"Oh, hey, no. I—you could come with me. If you want, I mean."

She tipped her head sideways and scrunched her nose in a way Kenny deemed kind of cute. "You want me to come with you?"

Kenny stuffed his hands in his pockets and stared at the ground. "You make me feel more confident, Jacqui."

To prove it, he looked back up, into her eyes. They were dark brown, almost black like her hair. Opposite in every way of Lee. *Shit. Lee.* Jacqui read his thoughts.

"All right then," said Jacqui, "let's go see the woman stupid enough to let a guy like you go."

This time, she led the lagging Kenny who suddenly suffered a bout of uncertainty. Twenty-four hours ago, all Kenny's thoughts revolved around winning back his wife. Something had changed, and it wasn't just his appearance.

As Jacqui chattered to him over her shoulder, Kenny considered his life. Had he been unhappy and not realized it? The answer struck him not like a bolt of lightning, but with a nine-volt jolt. Just enough to make him jump and hiss out a swear.

He *had* been miserable, and so had Lee. Misery, disguised as contentment, had run through their marriage like an underground river, flowing unobserved and unchecked. Layers of responsibilities, commitments, and obligations piled on like earth and sediment, piled higher and higher.

Get up at six-fifteen, jog five miles, shower, go to work, clock out, eat the dinner set in front of him—even though he hated cod and missed red meat—dry the dishes, take out the trash. Grade papers in bed under the adjustable bed lamp, go to bed.

Pay bills, host cookouts, chaperone dances, attend association meetings. Vote in local and national elections, pay taxes.

Feed the cat, try to make a baby. Try again. And again. And again. Try until making love is a chore. Try even when trying brought no pleasure, no connectiveness, no affection. Try, when you know it'll only bring more tears, more hollowness, more loneliness.

Jesus. Had it been that bleak? He didn't know it then, but he sure did now. The business of middle-class suburban life had too consumed them to notice. It took Lee's misdiagnosis to wake her up, and her leaving to awaken him from that long complacent slumber.

Kenny allowed himself to think about his future life, and what it might look like without Lee in it. Would they sell the house? Divide the assets? Would they fight over who kept Dexter? He doubted it, that cat had preferred Kenny from day one. Still, Lee might—

"Hello? Earth to Kenny. I said, they probably went in there."

Kenny followed her coral-painted, pointed finger to a thatch-roofed building with the name Cappy's spelled out in jaunty teal and white script above the door. Acoustic music drifted out each time the door opened, as did the smell of fried seafood.

Kenny had no fondness for the beach and had only gone for Lee's sake. He detested the insidious sand that no matter how well he rinsed and shook out, the gritty particles still found their way into his hair, the car, and even his mouth.

Married to his dislike of the shoreline existed an abhorrence for establishments that not only had sand in them but welcomed it. His sentiments toward fried seafood held equal low esteem as the rest. He grimaced.

"Gross," sniffed Jacqui, "I can't stand places like this. All that damn sand, it gets in everything. Don't even get me started on the seafood smell. Guess I'll have to wash my hair again tonight."

Kenny's jaw went slack as he looked at this short, voluptuous kindred spirit. He managed an emphatic nod.

"Hate to burst your balloon, but you've gotta do something here. Can't just stand outside. You ready for this?"

She gave a light tug on his sleeve and tipped her head again in that way that Kenny's stomach tighten and his palms tingle.

"I think so." He blinked, then said, "Bubble." He looked back at the restaurant door.

"Are you having a stroke? What bubble?"

"No, you said, 'burst your balloon.' The saying is burst your bubble."

"Is it? Huh. Whatever, I like balloon better. Never mind that, now. Stand up straight. Remember, you're Ryan fucking Gosling, damn it.

Now go in there and—" she faltered, "and get your wife back."

Kenny opened his mouth to speak, but Jacqui shoved him forward. He let her push him along. He didn't know what he'd have said, anyhow.

Kenny heard Lee's voice before he pinpointed her location. Even then, his brain couldn't comprehend. His wife—or an alternate universe version of her—sat in a stool beside the guitar man on a small stage. They turned their bodies towards each other and shared a microphone. Kenny saw only Lee's profile, and it looked radiant.

The man strummed the guitar and as he sang, he gazed into Lee's eyes in a way that made Kenny feel like he just walked in on them making love. Everything about what he saw on that stage made Kenny feel like he might vomit, yet he watched on.

He heard a pop—an actual balloon pop—and suddenly realized he'd been having his balloons burst quite a lot the last day or so. In times of crisis, Kenny reverted to his analytical nature.

He computed that he didn't feel jealous or angry. He felt numb, detached as he replayed the undoing of his marriage. The official one, not the slow burn one underneath the domesticity of their previous existence.

I want a divorce, Kenny. POP

You're under arrest. POP

The realization he hadn't been happy in years. Another *POP*. The last balloon in his hand, the one that had, 'Get Your Wife Back' written on it in black permanent marker popped the loudest when Lee and that man sang *that* song together.

It was a Kenny Loggins song Guitar Guy sang— Danny's Song, he recognized with a wave of nausea—and Lee leaned in to harmonize on the chorus. Her hand rested on the man's knee. They smiled at one another.

Kenny didn't know what they did or how they looked at the end of the song because he'd turned and walked back out the door, his feet carrying him to the beach because he didn't know where else to go.

"Kenny! Hey, wait up."

Jacqui stumbled and grabbed his forearm. He looked down, bewildered. He'd forgotten all about her.

"Sorry—I—are you all right?"

"I'm in high heels on the beach, Kenny. What do you think?" She looked up at his face and softened. "I'm fine. Hold me up while I take these things off."

Kenny obliged her awkwardly, putting his arm around her waist, then removing it to hold her arm, then holding her shoulders. She swore and held a finger up at him.

"Hang on. Just stay still. I'll hold your arm, don't move."

Once the buckles were undone, straps unstrapped, and heels off, Jacqui sighed and motioned him towards the shoreline.

"If you're going to make me go through all that, the least you can do is take me for a stroll along the damn beach. Better take your shoes off, too."

Kenny looked down at his laced-up, brown Dr. Martins. They were the most expensive shoes he owned. He'd debated for weeks over the purchase, scoured the internet for the best price, and read all the reviews. Lee's migraines had begun right around that same time.

"Lee, I found them," he said one night in bed. "Just ordered them and they'll be here by Thursday."

"Dr. Kerns ordered another MRI and some other tests. I may have a brain tumor, Kenny."

He'd connected those shoes to her migraines, despite knowing it was irrational. Even so, he'd kept them. It was *practical* to do so. Even though every time he looked at them and thought, *'The brain tumor shoes,'* he wore the damn things with a doggedness of a man who'd spent too much money on something not to use it. Kenny *hated* those shoes. The force of the feeling took him by surprise.

"I hate these shoes," he said aloud.

Jacqui blinked at the shoes, then at him. "So, toss them, then. Better yet, here, give them to me."

Kenny loosened and then kicked them off. He handed the pair to her and watched in bemusement as she looked up and down the beach and the street behind them.

"Ah-ha. Stay right there."

She dashed on her tiptoes to an elderly man pushing a metal shopping cart full of aluminum cans and plastic bottles. Gesturing, smiling, and even pointing in Kenny's direction once, she placed the shoes in the man's outstretched hands and waved over her shoulder as she ran back to Kenny. Lee would never have done something like that. Not because she wasn't generous, but because she abhorred germs and strangers with equal vehemence.

"Did you just give away my shoes?" Kenny laughed.

"Yup. We'll get you new ones. Ones with no bad memories attached."

Kenny looked down at the sand between his now bare toes. "How'd you know?"

Jacqui rolled her eyes. "Please, there isn't a woman alive who doesn't understand the purge. Now, come on, walk with me, talk with me. Tell me what the hell just happened back there."

Kenny did. He told her everything, starting from the day he met Lee Merriweather, to the day she became Lee Harper, to the migraines, the brain tumor fear, and at last, to the guitar man and his wife looking so made for each other.

"And that song? Of all songs. How could she sing that song after…?" He let the sentence fade.

They'd reached a pier and stood close, but not touching.

"I had a miscarriage, too. Four years ago. My fiancé—ex-fiancé—didn't want me to have it. Guess he got his wish."

Her voice was steady, calm even. But her hands gripped the railing hard enough to turn her knuckles white. Kenny covered one of her hands with his and said nothing.

After a few minutes of watching the ocean sway and pelicans fly, she said, "Kenny?"

"Yes?"

"It's fucking hot out here. Can we go get you some damn clothes now?"

They started with a pair of sandals for Kenny and flip-flops for Jacqui, and after putting nearly three-hundred dollars on his credit card, they wandered into a bar along the strip.

"My treat, Kenny," said Jacqui. "You've spent enough money for today, I'm sure."

Kenny looked at all the bags. It was true, he'd never spent that much money on clothes in one shot. At least he didn't think he did. Lee had done all their clothes shopping. Jacqui had stared at him in disbelief when he didn't know his pants size. Then she'd mortified him by grabbing the waistband of his pants and flipping it down to read the tag.

She also asked him—*asked*, not told—to model each outfit she'd tossed over the changing room door, giving thumbs up to those she approved and raspberries to the ones she didn't like.

The last one he tried on—navy blue cargo shorts and a pale pink polo—she jumped up, tore the price tags off, and begged him to wear it for the day.

Lee always expected him to wear whatever she picked out for him. Jacqui made him feel like he had a say in the matter, and even insisted that it was up to him. She meant it, too. Instead of pouting and getting angry when he didn't like something she said, 'Okay, back to the drawing board,' or 'No worries, we'll figure out your style.'

When he expressed his surprise at her easy acceptance, she laughed a humorless chortle.

"Jesus, Kenny. You're a grown-ass man, not a boy. Don't be afraid to assert yourself. In fact, I think it's sexy as hell when a man knows what he wants and goes for it."

Her words had been on repeat in his head since they'd left the store. More so after they'd downed a second round of drinks. Kenny wasn't much of a drinker. The same six-pack of IPA had sat in the back of the refrigerator for months, untouched until Lee helped herself to it. The martinis Jacqui ordered them were a lot stronger than pale ale.

I think it's sexy as hell when a man knows what he wants and goes for it.

"Kenny? Are you—"

Jacqui didn't get to finish the question because Kenny lips were on hers. At first, she kissed him back, letting her mouth melt under his. But as abruptly as the kiss began, it ended with her jumping to her feet and leaving Kenny mid-pucker. A man at the bar laughed and muttered, '*Smooth, buddy,*' loud enough for Kenny to hear. He didn't care, though.

"Jacqui, I'm sorry. I shouldn't have—"

"No, you shouldn't have."

Seeing the other patron's eyes on them, she stepped back to the table and sat down, pulling him down with her.

She leaned in and hissed, "It's not that I don't want you to kiss me, Kenny. Isn't it obvious that I like you?" At his surprised expression, she said, "Jesus. I *like* you, okay? But you're a mess. And you're married."

"Getting divorced, though."

"Yeah, a fact you've barely wrapped your brain around. Four hours ago, you got a makeover to win your wife back. Two hours ago, you walked into a restaurant to see her with another man. I've played rebound girl before, Kenny. It not a good feeling."

"But this isn't—you're not—"

"It is, and I am. At least I'm smart enough to see it faster this time. You're a great guy from what I can tell. If I met you at another time, I'd snatch you up before anyone else could."

Kenny saw the flicker of uncertainty followed by regret cross her face as she stood again.

"It's been nice spending time with you. If you're ever around this way again..."

She touched his shoulder, smiled sadly, and left him. He stared at their martini glasses—his half-empty, hers half-full—feeling confused and light-headed. Someone sat down across from him. A wild sense of hope that it was Jacqui returning made him look up with the beginnings of a smile. It was the man who had muttered under his breath.

"If you're coming over here to make fun of me, just leave me alone."

"Not at all, man. In fact, I'm here to commiserate. I've gotten pretty unceremoniously dumped recently myself. Twice you could say."

Kenny chuckled and said, "Me too, actually."

The man raised his beer, Kenny raised his martini glass, and they clinked them together.

"A martini, huh? Let me guess, lady's choice? Hang on I'll get you a man's drink." He twisted around to the bartender. "Hey, Jonny boy, grab another round of these, will you?" He turned back to Kenny and said, "The name's Nick. Nick Keller."

Kenny, matching the tone, said, "Harper. Kenny Harper.

Nick Keller squinted at Kenny. "Harper? Any relation to a Tenley Harper?"

"Yes, that's my wife."

"Your... *wife*?"

"Yep."

"Impossible."

"Fact."

The two men stared hard at each other. Nick tried again.

"Your wife is *Tenley* Harper? Blonde hair, gorgeous, a real pain in the ass?"

"Yep, that about sums her up."

Nick shook his head and took a short swig of beer before setting the bottle down hard on the table. "We can't be talking about the same chick."

Kenny scratched his chin. "Well, I doubt there are two Tenley's in the world. At least not in the same town. The odds are stacked too high against it."

Nick couldn't accept it. "How old is she? Your Tenley, I mean."

"Thirty-six."

"Shit," said Nick. "You got a picture of her on your phone? Show—"

"Nick! Are you kidding me right now? I give you another chance and you do this *again*?"

A leggy blonde loomed over the table, her hands on her hips. Nick swore under his breath, then plastered a bright smile on his face.

"Chantelle, babe, I've been looking all over for you, but you disappeared."

"Is that so, Nick? Because it looks to me like you're sitting in a bar, drinking with some guy—"

"His name is Kenny. Kenny, meet Chantelle."

"Nice to meet—"

"While you've been sitting here, drinking with—"

"Kenny," said Kenny.

She stared at him a moment. "Right. Got it." Turning her glare back to Kenny's new friend, she said, "While you've been here getting drunk, I've been waiting in Bebe. *Where you left me* to 'go find the men's room.' An hour ago, Nick."

"I got a little side-tracked. What can I say?"

Chantelle's jaw dropped. She looked from Nick to Kenny in speechless disbelief. Kenny wanted to say something, but for the life of him, he couldn't think of anything. This seemed to infuriate her even more. He watched her look down at the half-full martini glass, then at Nick. They all knew what she was thinking of doing.

"Chantelle," said Nick, putting both hands up. "Don't do—"

She swept the glass up and dumped it over his head. Nick cringed but sat still for the abuse. When the last drop dripped on his head, she handed him the glass and leaned in close enough to kiss him.

"You're an asshole, Nick Keller. I'm going back to Miami. Lose my number." She pivoted with a flip of long hair in his face, then turned back, this time smiling at Kenny. A devilish gleam sparkled in her summer sky blue eyes.

"On second thought, give it to the Ryan Goslings look-a-like."

Some of the patrons in the bar applauded, one yelled, "There's a slow burn for ya, Keller."

The bartender tossed a roll of paper towels to Nick and shook his head. Kenny watched all in amazement. It was feeling like he'd stepped inside a soap opera. How had his life turned so bizarre in such a short time?

"All right, back to solving our little mystery," said Nick.

"A-a woman just dumped her drink on your head."

Nick waved him off. "It's fine. She'll be fine. Weekend fling. She'll go back to Miami, tell her girlfriends she had a great time, and call me in a month or two like nothing."

Nick felt around in his pockets, and his calm demeanor turned panicked.

"Everything okay?" Kenny sat forward.

Nick stood. "My car keys. Shit. She has my car keys in her purse. I gotta run, man. Listen, look me up on Facebook, we need to talk."

Kenny called out, "Will do," but Nick Keller had already dashed out the door in search of the angry Amazon and his car keys.

The break from all the constant action felt like a relief. Since Lee's announcement one day ago, Kenny's world had not just tilted, but broke off its axis. He needed to put it in order. And since Kenny Harper was a man who thrived on lists, he made a mental one in chronological order.

Lee went to her appointment—solo, at her insistence—expecting bad news. Instead, she received good news, which seemed to have prompted her to give Kenny a different bad news. Kenny left work, got arrested, met a drag queen, got a makeover by a beautiful woman who then took him to find his wife—who was now with another man in a bar—and clothes shopping. He kissed the woman, she left him, too. A stranger sits down, claims to know his wife. Man leaves Kenny.

Kenny's conclusion? He sure got left behind a lot all the sudden. The next thing he realized? He was getting really pissed off. There was a mirror across the way from where he sat. Again, he almost didn't recognize himself. The guy in the mirror looked stylish. Modern. Cool, even. If only he could feel the way he looked.

He pulled out his phone and typed 'Ryan Gosling' into the search tab, then clicked on 'videos.' After ordering another drink, he spent twenty minutes watching movie and interview clips of the man he semi-resembled—he still didn't see it, himself—he decided it was time to complete the Kenny transformation.

He called the waitress over. "Hey, s-sweetheart. I'll take the check now." Her eyebrow rose to a considerable height. "Or whenever you get a chance. Please. Thank you."

"Sure. I can grab that for you," said the waitress. She eyed him caustically, though.

Deciding not to be deterred, he winked at her. She rewarded him with a smile. She rolled her eyes with it, but it was still a smile.

As he waited, Kenny typed in 'hotels near me' in his phone's search box. It took a few tries. His fingers wouldn't type what his mind told them to. The first on the list—The Pink Flamingo Inn—proved within walking distance, had four stars, decent rates, and vacancy. They also had a 'book online and save' icon, so Kenny did.

Sure, he could've driven home and come back in the morning, but the thought of going back to the quiet, empty house held no appeal. Dexter, he knew, would be fine for a day. Lee kept his water and food bowls full, his litterbox fresh. Unless those things weren't up to his immovable standards, the cat couldn't care less whether his humans were home or not. Besides, he got the idea he might be a little intoxicated. Maybe a lot.

"Cats are especially independent. I-I'm independent, too," said Kenny to no one in particular. "I'm on my own, folks."

It dawned on him—in his bleary, hazy state—how readily his thoughts had turned to acceptance of his wife's abandonment. Had it been the sight of her with another man? Or, just as possible, did it have something to do with his attraction to Jacqui? Did flamingos really sleep with one leg up? Why hadn't he asked that Nick guy how he knew his wife?

The skippiness of his thoughts should have clued him in. He was drunk. Roaringly so, in fact. But Kenny had almost no experience with such a sensation, not since that one time in college, and that was on beer. Sure, he'd been loopy and even goofy, but this? This felt like standing one-legged on a trampoline, and he hadn't even stood up yet.

He signed the check under the watchful eye of the waitress. The paper blurred as he squinted at it. When Kenny looked up to hand her the slip, he discovered there were two of her.

"Ah, twins. Twins are nice," said Kenny.

He stood and the one-legged trampoline became something more like the suction of an undertow. His feet didn't want to stay underneath him, and his head felt like it was being shaken like a snow globe.

"Ah, shit," said the waitress—Dottie, according to her name tag.

Kenny knew this because his eyes were less than an inch away from the plastic rectangle clipped to her tank top. He didn't know that his hands were on her hips or that his nose pressed against the swell of her breast.

"Easy does it, Romeo."

She poked her index finger into his forehead and pushed his head back. Over her shoulder she called, "Jonny! We've got a floater, here."

A pair of hairy arms hooked under his armpits and dragged him into the recesses of the bar, around a corner, past men's and women's bathrooms, and into a square room with a desk, makeshift bookcase made from crates, and a loveseat with springs that squeaked when the hairy-armed person dropped him unceremoniously onto it.

"Well, that was a fun ride," said Kenny. The word 'ride' sounded funny to him. He repeated it several times.

The hairy man wiped his big, wrinkled forehead with the back of his black shirt. He breathed like he'd just run a marathon and stared at Kenny.

"You're heavier than you look, buddy. You been drinking all day or something? I know I only served you, what, two martinis? Maybe three? And Keller got you one beer. You can't be this fucked up just from that."

Kenny shrugged, or at least tried to. "I dunno. Whas in a martini, anyhow?"

The man cocked his head and looked at Kenny as if he were kidding. "Those were vodka martinis."

"Ah, well. There you have it, Hairy. I have an intolerance to vodka. It 'fucks me up' as one might say."

Kenny laughed and after a pause, so did hairy man. "Did you just call me Harry?"

"No, I called you *hairy*. That's different."

"Right," said the man named Jonny.

Kenny, somewhere in the coherent side of his mind, knew this but had simply forgotten.

"You got someone we can call to get you? You aren't driving anywhere for a while."

His first thought was Lee. She was off somewhere with her new boyfriend, Mr. Stinking Guitar Guy.

"I... don't know who guitar guy is, but—"

"I said that out loud, huh?" Kenny laughed again.

Jonny the bartender didn't laugh this time but looked at him with sympathy. "You got a relative or a friend I can call for you?"

Kenny thought. Chet? No way. He had no friends, no real ones at least. Then he remembered.

"Fuchsia! Can you call my friend Fuchsia?"

"Uh, sure. You got a number?"

Kenny dug around for his phone, found his new friend's number programmed in it, and handed it to hairy Jonny. Then he curled up in a ball and closed his eyes. Everything spun.

"One foot on the floor, newbie. It'll stop the spins." Into the phone, he said, "Yeah, is this... Fuchsia? Great. So, I got a buddy of yours here? Goes by the name Kenny? Yeah, that's the one. Anyhow, he's shit-housed and needs a lift."

Kenny felt like a Weimaraner trying to fit on a doll chair, but he didn't care. He gave Jonny a haphazard wave each time he glanced at him. Jonny continued the conversation.

"Yep, right on the main road. Left side. Can't miss it. Come up to the bar when you get here." He handed the phone to Kenny and said, "Your friend will be here in ten minutes. Don't touch anything, don't move, and for fuck's sake, if you're gonna puke, do it in the trashcan. Here."

He set waste bin on the floor by his head and Kenny gave him the thumbs up. Jonny didn't return the salutation as he left the office. The door opened and the music from the bar—Jimmy Buffett, they all played Jimmy Buffett—poured into the small room. When he closed it behind him, the music became muffled again.

Kenny blinked slowly at the corner of the sideways coffee table. His gaze shifted to the sideways desk and sideways print of the beach on the cracked plaster wall. His last coherent thought was, "Sand. So much sand." Then, Kenny either slept or passed out. He awoke to a strange man with a familiar voice staring at him in too close proximity. So close that Kenny could smell the minty gum on his breath.

"Hello," said Kenny. "Who are you?"

"Oh, Jesus, honey. It's Frank." Frank sighed. "It's me, Fuchsia."

"No, you're not," said Kenny. He picked his head up and squinted at the man. "You sound like Fuchsia, though."

"That's because I *am* Fuchsia, Kenny." To the bartender he said, "Damn, just how much did he drink?"

"Two martinis and a beer."

Frank who was also Fuchsia blinked. "Seriously?"

Kenny sat up. "It was three, thank you. I have a low tolerance for alcohol."

"No shit, Sherlock. Where's Jacqui?"

"I kissed her, and she left."

"You did? Well, good for you. So, why did she—"

"Hey, I hate to interrupt, but can you two take this somewhere else? I got a bar to run, you know?"

"Yeah, sure. Come on, Kenny. I'll take you to my place until you sober up."

"Oh, I got a room at the Pink Pelican. No, the Pink Flamingo. Or is it—"

"Well, cancel your reservation, Sunshine. I'm gonna get you straightened out." Frank laughed. "Now there's a sentence I've never said before."

"You're funny," said Kenny. He didn't know why they were laughing.

"Kenny, you can call me Frank. I'm not in drag right now."

Kenny's slow synapses finally fired. "Oh, right. I get it. You're Fuchsia when you're not Frank, and you're Frank when you're not Fuchsia."

"Atta boy, Kenny."

The mid-day sunshine had turned to dusk by the time Kenny left—he looked back at the sign—The Blue Parrot Bar.

"Hey, it's almost nighttime," said Kenny. His mouth hung open and his eyebrows shot up towards his hairline.

"You don't miss a trick, do you, big guy? When was the last time you ate, Kenny?"

Kenny scratched to top of his head. "This morning? Yeah, I think it was this morning."

Frank-Fuchsia *tsked* and shook his head. As Frank, Fuchsia looked like any other guy. Short blond hair, sun-tanned, the hint of stubble on his cheeks and jaw. He wore his sunglasses on top of his head, a retro panel shirt, baggy shorts, and brown sandals. Around his neck, a necklace made from tiny white seashells, and in both ears sets of small silver hoop earring.

"Stop staring, Kenny. Hop in, and we'll get you some food."

Frank motioned to a bright purple Jeep idling at the curb. There were no doors, windows—besides the windshield—and no top. He'd always wanted a Jeep, but Lee said they were too boxy and not comfortable to sit in. Kenny grinned. He felt better already. Then he puked out the window.

<u>14</u> JACQUI

Jacqui strode from the bar, from *Kenny*, with her head high and her spirits low. She *knew*. Damn it, she knew better than to get caught up in someone else's drama. But what did she do? She got involved. Worse, she knew she'd do it the minute Fuchsia brought that tall, goofy guy into the salon. Like a giraffe, he was. Big brown eyes blinking at her. She paused at the corner and looked back. He still sat where she'd left him, looking like a kicked puppy. She shook her head.

No, girl. Don't do it.

Jacqui always was a sucker for the tall ones. At five-three, it wasn't hard to find guys taller than her, but she loved *really* tall. Add brainiac to the mix? Hook, line and sinker, she'd be into him. If she wanted to get all Freudian about it, she suppose it had to do with her father. It always did, right?

Pasqual Franchione was tall, handsome and smart. At least that's what her mother always told her. He left when Jacqui was one, went back to Italy and never heard from again.

"He was in college, Jacqui. I worked in a factory. It was supposed to be a summer fling, nothing more. We were never meant to last."

Her mother knew Pasqual planned to return to Italy–knew it all along–but it didn't stop her for falling for the smoldering good looks and elegant accent. When she found out she was pregnant, he did the right thing and married her. They were too different, though. Their worlds clashed instead of melding.

He wanted to talk about physics and engineering, she wanted to talk about her garden and the neighbors. They bored each other. When he left, he said it was to visit family and that he'd return in a month. Maria knew better, though.

"Why'd you let him leave, then," asked Jacqui once.

Maria shrugged, "We'd been in love with the idea of one another. Not each other. I wanted more, he wanted more."

Neither had considered the effect his absence would have on their daughter. It was a bitter pill to swallow for Jacqui, knowing this. Several shitty relationships and two therapists later, she had a grip on it all. She understood *the psychology of her choices*, as Dr. Jen liked to say.

It was Dr. Jen's voice in her head that stopped the kiss between her and Kenny.

"Are you sure this is something that can bring joy to your life, Jacqui? Are you seeing the pattern? Tall, smart, handsome...and unavailable. He's *married*."

And up until a half hour ago, I was helping him win back his wife.

The answer was clear. Kenny Harper, no matter how cute or how sweet he was, could not bring joy to her life. Therefore, Jacqui walked away. That didn't mean it was easy, though. She kept picturing his face as she walked back to the salon. Dejected, confused... endearing.

They'd related on so many levels, too. That was the part that saddened her the most. There was a real sense of—of… connection. She told him about her miscarriage. No one besides Jacqui and her ex knew about that, and she'd shared it with Kenny. It wasn't like her to do that, to expose her wounds and be vulnerable.

He'd made it easy, though. Kenny Harper was so open, so without guile, that Jacqui found herself doing the same. How could his wife not appreciate such an amazing guy? He threw away expensive shoes because they reminded him of something sad. Talk about sensitivity. Talk about undervalued was more like it.

A guy like Kenny, wasted on a woman who didn't value a decent man. It made her mad. No, it made her pissed the hell off. At him, at her, at Fuchsia for bringing him in. At her father all over again—just because—and at last, at herself.

She'd unlocked the salon in a daze and sat on one of the styling chairs. Her hair had frizzed from the heat and her makeup needed refreshing. When Jacqui stood again, the grit of beach sand crunched under her soles. It made her sad all over again.

The bell above the door chimed and three teenage girls burst in, laughing and shoving each other.

"Oh, sorry," said one. "Are you, like, open, or..."

"The sign says closed, stupid," said one of the friends to the first girl.

Jacqui sighed then put on a smile. "Come on in, girls. I'm open."

They came in like colts with their long, tan limbs and flowing manes and pored over hairstyle books and magazines on the table. Jacqui tied her apron and lined its front pouch with scissors and combs, watching them from the corner of her eye.

Two of the girls held up pictures and spoke in that maternal tone most girls are born knowing to the third. She was a pretty, strawberry-blonde haired girl with sad, doe-like almond eyes. Each hairstyle the showed her—saying 'how about this one' or 'oh, look,' every time—she either shrugged or shook her head. The girl who'd asked if the salon was open caught Jacqui looking.

"She just broke up with her boyfriend," said the girl, wagging her thumb at her sad-eyed friend.

Jacqui said, "Ah, I see. Makeover therapy, then?"

"Exactly. I'm Jennie, that's Marina, and this is poor Annabelle."

"Not *poor* Annabelle," admonished the one named Marina. "*Lucky* Annabelle for breaking up with that two-timing jerk."

Poor—or lucky—Annabelle looked at Jacqui and nodded. "He was seeing a girl from camp. I saw it on Snapchat."

"Belle, I tried to warn you about him," said Marina, "bad boys are just bad news. You have to go for the good guys."

"Oh, come off it, Mar," said Jennie. "Every girl loves a bad boy. That's just the way it is. Like, tell me you would turn Jason Mamoa away. Puh-lease." Jennie added an eye roll to emphasis her point.

"Shows what you know. Jason Mamoa is *not* a bad boy. He just *looks* like one." She held up her fist and counted off the qualities that made the actor in question a 'good guy.' "One. He's environmentally conscious. Two. He's, like, totally, madly in love with his wife. And three, he's a dad," said Marina.

Both Jacqui and Annabelle stayed quiet. She couldn't know what the young girl thought, but she guessed it was a hope that the other two would just shut up about Jason Mamoa. As they continued their argument, Jacqui caught Annabelle's eye and nodded to the waiting chair.

"Thanks for taking me in," said Annabelle.

"Sure thing sweetie. Sorry about the boyfriend situation."

Jacqui almost added one of those cliché quotes. Something like, 'the right guy is out there' or 'plenty of fish in the sea,' but she thought better of it. Who was *she* to give advice, anyhow? Besides, what she really wanted to say to those girls was, 'Guess what, kids? Even the good guys will break your heart.'

Then she'd have three sad, crying girls in her salon. And one sad, crying adult. So, she kept her pessimistic thoughts to herself and instead complimented them for being such good friends to each other.

"Yeah, we've been besties since, like, forever," said Jennie.

Marina added, "Yeah, we have each other's backs. No matter what."

Annabelle smiled and said, "Even when we don't agree."

They reminded Jacqui of something else she didn't have. A group of girlfriends like what those girls had. Maybe she needed to spend less time trying to find a guy, and more time working on the friendships she'd let drift apart. And making new ones, too.

By the time she sent the girls on their way, Jacqui had resolved to put things in better perspective. Kenny was a good guy and maybe he'd come around again or maybe he wouldn't. Either way, she was going to live her life to the fullest. No apologies, on her conditions, and for herself.

She stared in the mirror. "From now on, girl."

15 TEN

The ocean always had a way of centering Ten. The briny air, the call of the gulls, the ebb and flow of the tide. Low tide was her favorite, when she could walk out far and look back at the house from a distance.

Years ago, when Ten was still a teen, Charlie had put out a small lighthouse statue from which a soft light carried, as if to guide her home. She could walk for miles in either direction along the beach, but when she spotted the lighthouse light, she knew home was near.

It was dusk, and Ten had places she needed to be and people she meant to see, but the sea called her, and she couldn't resist her pull. She'd already dressed for Cappy's—a soft, flowing white dress, strappy sandals, her hair in a long, loose braid—but now the sandals lie in the sand and the breeze pulled her hair free.

The hem of her skirt soaked in the saltwater as the ripples tickled her ankles and the wet sand sucked at her feet. She didn't fight it. The sun sink towards the water and she hugged her arms around her waist. How many more of these sunsets would she get? Because there could never, ever in a million years be enough. Sometimes she wasn't sure if she believed there was a God, but in moments like this, Ten believed with all her heart.

"If you *are* up there... if you're listening, maybe you could give me a chance? I know I haven't done enough with the one I've been given. Hell, maybe I've lived kind of a selfish life. I realize that. But as far as I know, I've done little harm."

Tenley blanched. Was she trying to bullshit God? She tried again. "Okay, listen, I know. I'm selfish, I drink too much, I sleep around, I avoid confrontation. And responsibility. And commitment. And a bunch of other things, too. But I can do better. I can *be* better. Just... give me another chance, please?"

She wasn't sure what to do next. Say Amen? Bow? She settled on saying thank you, then turned back to the shore. A man stood at the water's edge, his hands in his pockets and looking in her direction. He was too far to make out, but Ten had her suspicions who it was. The man raked his hand through his hair, confirming her guess. *Nick Keller.* She took her time getting to him.

When she reached him, she asked, "What are you doing here?"

"I wanted to talk to you, Harper."

"Nick, haven't we already said everything there is to say?"

She'd wanted the words to sound cold, indifferent, but to her own ears, she sounded tired and resigned. He, too, seemed surprised. His gaze narrowed as he studied her face. She looked away, flustered by his intense stare.

"What's going on with you, Harper? You're usually in party mode by this time on a Friday."

"Nothing's *going on* with me, Keller. And if there *was* something, it'd be none of your concern."

None of your business. That's what she *should* have said. It as what she'd meant.

"Yesterday, outside Cappy's, you said, *I'm not ready yet*. Ready for what, Ten?"

They'd always been Harper and Keller. No first names, just last. Hearing her name from his lips affected her more than she could believe.

If Margot were there, she'd snort and say Ten was full of shit and she'd always had a thing for Nick Keller. She supposed it was true. Not that it mattered after his book published. Nor did it matter now since she'd be dead in a few months. The morbid thought sobered her.

"Not ready for Nick Keller to stalk me, that's what."

She passed him, kicking up sprays of water behind her. She felt the heat of him close behind but tried to ignore it.

"You're not fooling me, Harper. Something's up with you. Let someone in for once. Let *me* in."

She stopped but didn't face him. They'd never been together, yet it felt like he knew her as intimately as a lover. Ten wanted to step back into his arms and she also wanted to spin around and punch him in the gut. She wanted to feel something, and she wanted to feel nothing.

"You want in, Keller? Fine." Ten faced him. "I'm dying. Doctor gave me six months. Maybe ten. Welcome *in*."

Nick stepped back. "The fuck, Harper. Not even remotely funny. Jesus."

He ran a hand through his hair and frowned at her. Ten hadn't said another word. She just stared at him.

"You're joking, right? You *have* to be joking. Harper, you're not—you're not fucking *dying*."

"Wish I were joking, Keller, but I'm not. You're the only one who knows, so, I'd appreciate you keeping your big mouth shut." She threw her head back and laughed at the sky. "What am I saying? I just told Mister Tell-All to keep a secret. I must be—"

Nick grabbed her arms and pulled her against him. He wrapped her in a tight hug and rested his cheek on the top of her head. Ten tensed; her arms rigid at her sides. Maybe it was the smell of his cologne, or the heat, or maybe it was the damn brain tumor, but God help her, she put her arms around his back and let him hold her.

The sounds of another couple passed them by, laughing and splashing one another in the shallow surf. The spell broke and Ten pulled out of his arms. Vulnerability and self-consciousness were not feelings she'd ever been accustomed with, but she recognized them quick enough to know she didn't like it.

"Ten, I—"

"No need to make this a big thing, Keller. Thanks for the... support. I'd appreciate you keeping this on the down-low until I've told Charlie."

"Wait, your *father* doesn't know? Harper, you gotta—"

Her eyes became slits and her tone turned sharp. "I don't *gotta* anything, Keller. This isn't your problem, so don't worry."

"Jesus, Harper. Are you really that thick? I'm fucking crazy about you. Have been since the day we met. Shit, before that."

His hand went to his hair again. The Keller distress signal. Next, he'd shove his hands in his pockets, thumbs out and looped around the waistband. Funny how well she knew his mannerisms and gestures. She'd known he liked her back when, too. But the last part? That was new.

"Before? What do you mean before? I don't remember ever meeting you before you showed up on our doorstep looking for a story."

To Ten's shock, Nick turned bashful. "Ah, I— never mind, all right? It's stupid."

Ten waited; arms crossed over her chest.

He huffed. "Okay, fine. Obviously, you know I loved pro wrestling when I was a kid. I followed all the big names, especially Charlie The Hurricane Harper. So, when I heard the Wrestling Champs of America was in town, and Vance Vincent was interviewing the wrestlers, I waited for it to come on tv."

He stopped. Ten, brow raised in anticipation, said, "Go on, Keller."

"Instead of announcing Hurricane, he introduced *you*. Out walks this skinny, wild-haired girl—like the chick from the Blue Lagoon movie, or something—and my jaw dropped. You were so *cool*."

Ten laughed and shook her head. Her tension from moments before dissipated, at least a little. Something about a vulnerable, open Nick Keller enticed her to hear more. They walked along the beach and Nick continued.

"I didn't have the vocabulary for it then—shit, I was, fifteen—but it wasn't just that you were gorgeous. The cameras didn't faze you; the questions didn't affect you. You were so self-possessed. I-I'd never seen anyone like you."

"I remember that interview. The guy was kind of a jerk. He showed my dad and I the questions before the show, but he left off the one about my mother. Charlie was pissed. That was the last interview I ever did."

"Yeah, I know," said Nick.

"Nick Keller, you *are* a creepy stalker. I knew it."

Ten wasn't freaked out but flattered. And amused. That didn't stop her from wanting to make him squirm a little more.

"So, you don't have, like, a Tenley Harper shrine in your closet or anything, do you? Or a room filled with pictures of me? That'd be fucked up, Keller."

"I knew I shouldn't have told you."

"Relax, I'm fucking with you. It's sweet. I think. Maybe I'll just text Margot and let her know where I am and who I'm with in case I turn up missing."

"Nice, really nice Har—"

"Shit. Margot. I was supposed to meet her and the gang at Cappy's. I gotta go, Nick."

Nick smiled.

"What? Why are you smiling all goofy like that, weirdo?"

"You called me Nick. I don't think I've ever heard you say my name, Harper."

"Yeah, well don't get used to it, Kell—"

His kiss cut her off. Ten saw it coming and she let it happen. *Just once.* She had to steel herself against this, this *craziness*. It was pointless because—

"I'm dying, Nick. Remember? There's no point. This can't go anywhere." She pulled back. "Unless that's your twisted idea of the perfect relationship. Hook up with a woman you know can't be around long term? Say all the things I want to hear because, hey, why not? You won't have to follow through on anything."

Nick still had a hand coiled in her hair. He let it slip out and dropped it to his side. His soft gaze turned hard.

"Nice, Harper. Really fucking nice. Is that what you think?"

"I don't *know* what to think. I can't even—"

"Your friends are waiting for you, Harper. I'll, uh, we'll talk soon."

Before another word could leave her lips, Nick Keller turned and walked away. Even as she told herself it was for the best, her heart squeezed, and her eyes stung. Ten spun on her heel, grabbed her sandals and ran in the opposite direction of Nick Keller. Damn him and his crazy confessions.

16 NURSE MARIA

Maria Rodriguez parked in her usual spot at the medical office. She was three shades darker from the Aruba sun and five pounds heavier from the resort food. Or, more likely, the daily Pina coladas.

She craned her neck at the brick building from behind her steering wheel and frowned. "Back to reality, Maria."

The elevator door opened onto the third floor, home of Dr. Malcom Kerns & Dr. Keaton Rue, Doctors of Internal Medicine and General Practice. As if she'd never left, Maria began her morning routine. Unlock doors, turn on lights, power up computers, printers, and fax. Make coffee. Put lunch in the refrigerator.

As she waited for the coffee to brew, Maria rechecked the office for signs of things out of place. The temp had done a decent job. Nothing out of order and the fridge had even been cleaned out before the weekend.

"Impressive," said Maria. "Now, what do my files look like, I wonder?"

At her desk, coffee in hand and eye on the clock, Maria opened the scheduler. Both doctors weren't due in for another hour and the answering service would pick up calls for thirty more minutes, which meant Maria could catch up on everything in relative peace and quiet.

When her cell phone rang, she nearly jumped out of her chair.

"Babe, what are you calling so early for?"

"I just miss you already, that's all," said Maria's husband.

Maria laughed. "Aw, I miss you, too. Let's go back to Aruba. Screw our jobs."

"Nurse Rodriguez?"

Maria jumped once again, swore under her breath and said, "Babe, I gotta go. Bye."

She forced a smile and said, "Dr. Rue, I wasn't—you're here early. I hope the temp didn't—"

"I have some unfortunate news, Maria. Would you come down to my office?"

"Oh. Of course, Dr. Rue. Can I grab you a coffee?"

Why did you offer to get him coffee? You're not a waitress, Maria.

She hated how nervous he made her feel. Dr. Kerns never made her feel like that. Such a sweet man. Why he ever partnered with Dr. Stick in the Mud, she'd never understand.

"Thank you. Black, one sugar."

You would *say yes.*

Dr. Kerns would've said, 'I'll grab it myself,' and offered to refresh hers while he was at it. The pause gave her time to wonder if she were in trouble. Maria was excellent at her job and took great pride in it. She put herself through nursing school, paid off her student loans in record time, and landed a job in private practice.

Her indignation rose. If he was going to come at her with some petty complaint—forgetting to take her yogurt out of the fridge before she left for vacation, or something—she would remind him of all she does.

Maria was still running down a mental list of her kudos while she set his mug on the desk and stood before him, her back straight and hands tight around her cup.

"Have a seat, Maria. Please."

Maria gave a curt nod and sat. Dr. Rue removed his wire-rimmed glasses, closed his eyes, and squeezed the bridge of his nose.

Oh, my God, he's going to fire me. That's what this is about. They must've liked the temp better, and—

"I'm afraid I have some sad news. Dr. Kerns passed away while you were gone."

Maria thought she heard him say Dr. Kerns was dead, but that couldn't be. Could it?

"I'm sorry, did you say *Dr. Kerns*... He *died*?"

"Yes. His flu progressed to pneumonia. By the time they'd brought him to the hospital, it was too late. Ironic, I'm sure."

"Oh, my God. He was such a good man. His poor wife. His poor family."

"He was quite fond of you. As am I, Maria. I hope you'll be willing to stay on? Things will be hectic until we find another physician to take his—

well, to join the practice. I'll be giving you a raise, naturally."

"I—thank you, Dr. Rue. I'm happy to stay on."

"You say that now. Maybe decide after I tell you we'll be working late tonight to go over Dr. Kerns cases and files."

Maria deflated, but only a little. A raise would mean she and Luis would be that much closer to buying a house and starting their family.

"It's no problem at all, Dr. Rue. Once I get today's schedule all set, I'll start pulling files."

"Much appreciated. Let's start with most recent patients and work our way backward, yes?"

Maria nodded.

"Oh, and, I hope this means you won't be saying *screw this job* and go back to Aruba."

Dr. Rue smiled. Maria blushed and stammered her apologies. He waved her off good-naturedly and Maria walked away with a new, tentatively hopeful outlook on her future.

<u>17 LEE</u>

Max studied Lee's face with concern. "You still have that headache?"

They'd finished breakfast on the lanai, then went for a stroll along the beach with Jude galloping across the sand as the sun climbing higher in the sky. Almost two weeks of near constant companionship, daily sex, music, great wine, and Lee only wanted more of the same. A nagging headache would not spoil their fun if she could help it.

"It's nothing, really. Nothing a couple ibuprofen won't fix. Are you sure you want me to sing again? This is your thing. I'd hate to—"

"Lee, sweetheart, I *need* you up there with me. Everyone loves a duo. Besides, it opens a whole new catalogue of music. Stuff I've been dying to try."

Max slung an arm over her shoulders and panned the other across the sky as if reading a marque. "Max & Lee Live. Or maybe, Max & Lee Acoustic. Which did you like better?"

She gazed up at his warm, rugged face. Could something this wonderful last? God, she hoped so. "I like them both. I'm just happy to be here. With *you*, Max."

Max kissed her nose. 'Me, too, little lady." His took a deep breath. "Listen. I know—I *believe* you're running from something. Or someone? Just—it's not the law, is it? I mean, you're not a wanted felon or anything, right?"

"Oh, Max, no. Nothing so dramatic. I just needed to change my life, that's all."

This is the moment, Lee. Tell him you're married.

"Good. Thank God. The only thing worse than you being an ax murderer is married." He laughed. "But I checked for a ring the day we met. All clear."

"Max, I—" She couldn't do it. "I think I'd like to take a nap before we go to Cappy's if you don't mind?"

"That headache still bothering you, huh? Let's get you back home."

Home.

The ring of his cell phone spared Lee from saying anything more. As they walked back to the house, she contemplated how she'd break the news—*news he considered worse than dating an ax murderer*—to him and only half-listened to his end of the conversation.

"Hey, kid. What's up?" Pause. "Ah, he missed his buddies this morning, too." A pause followed by a burst of laughter. "Oh, Jude will love that. So. what's the favor?"

Max covered the mouthpiece and whispered, "Sorry, babe. It's my dog walker. Just be a minute."

Lee smiled and motioned it was no problem. The longer she had to think, the better.

Max listened, then said, "Aw, kid, I'm honored. What time is the party? Sounds great. Hey, mind if I bring my girl with me?" Max winked at Lee. "Yes, you've heard correctly. She's all that and more."

More banter volleyed, from which Lee gathered that they were invited to both sing and be guests at a party for his dog walker's father. And something about a hurricane, which she didn't understand.

"Sorry about that," said Max.

"So, I gather we're going to a party? Unless you call someone else your girl."

"You're the only one for me, Lee."

"Aw, you're sweet—"

"No, I mean it." Max stopped and took her hands. "Lee, I haven't felt this way about a woman since... since my wife. I never thought I *could* feel this way again. You've brought me back to life."

Lee stammered, but no words came out.

"Have I scared you away now? I'm sorry. I just—"

"Max?"

"Yes?"

"Shut up and kiss me."

He did, silencing all conversation. They walked on, leaving wet footprints in the sand behind Jude's. Lee didn't need to look back to know the incoming tide erased their imprints almost immediately. As if they'd never been there at all.

<u>18 TEN</u>

"Sweetheart, you don't have to throw me a party. It's too much trouble."

"Daddy, we're having the party of all parties for you, and that's final."

Ten shifted the cardboard box of decorations to her hip, planted a kiss on her father's cheek, then dropped the box on the kitchen island with a thud.

"What the hell's in there, a dead body?"

"Ha ha, funny. No, it's all the stuff from that pig roast we had a few years ago. At least I think it is. The label's worn off. Anyhow, I thought we'd have a luau theme."

"Luau, huh? I wouldn't mind getting—"

"Do not say—"

"Lei-ed."

"Gross, Dad. TMI."

Charlie gave a hearty laugh at his daughter's mortification. "Oh, now when did you become so prim and proper?"

"When my sixty-five-year-old father started making lei jokes."

"I'm still sixty-four, smart ass. At least for another forty-eight hours, I am. So, who's coming? You invite any of your friends?"

Ten slanted a suspicious eye at her father, "Anyone in particular you mean?"

Charlie shrugged but looked away.

"Daddy? Do you want me to invite *Margot*? I mean, I planned on it anyhow, but—"

"Oh, well, if you planned on it then, there you have it. Doesn't make a difference."

His nonchalance was so put on that Ten gaped at him. "All right, Charlie Harper. Fess up. What's going on here?"

"Nothing," said Charlie, an octave higher than normal. Seeing his daughter had no intention of letting it go, he slumped in his seat and said, "She stopped by the other day, looking for you. Guess you bailed on dinner, or something? Anyhow, we got to talking, that's all. No big deal."

"You *got to talking?*"

"And had a couple glasses of wine."

"You got to talking *and* you drank wine together? Interesting. Just how long did you two talk for? All the lights were out when I got home."

"Well, not all our talking happened downstairs."

Ten waved her hands and stepped back. "Ew. Stop. No more. Enough said. I have to find the tiki torches."

Before Charlie could add another nauseated detail about his and Margot's *conversation*, Ten dashed out of the house to the garage for more decorations. The task gave her time to think.

Dad and Margot, trying again after all these years.

The timing couldn't have been more perfect. When Ten died, he'd at least have someone by his side. To know her dad had at long last found love... well, it made dying—and the hiding of the fact— slightly less awful.

Every morning, she looked in the mirror to see if she looked different. Was she paler? No. Thinner?

No. Should she be calling her doctor? Should he have called *her* by now? That doctor who'd seen her that awful day wasn't her cup of tea. No bedside manner at all. She'd have to ask for that Kerns guy again, the one Lucy recommended. Maybe he had something better to say than, 'Sorry you're dying. Bye now.'

Ten set the armload of torches by the pool house and went back inside. Charlie was shoving an envelope in his back pocket and folding the flaps of the box back in place. He sprang back like he'd had his hand in the cookie jar before dinner.

"Dad? What's that?"

She thrust her chin toward his hand as he tried to stuff it far in the pocket of his shorts. The Parkinson's made the move difficult.

"Wh-what's what. Oh, nothing. Just, ah, you—"

Ten screwed her face up, half laughing at her father, half-baffled by his behavior. Then she remembered his penchant for *giving* gifts on his birthday. The envelope likely had show tickets, or maybe even plane tickets, a surprise for her.

"Ah, ha. I bet I have an idea. Hand it over, old man. The jig is up."

Despite his protestations and attempt to keep the paper from her grasp, Ten snagged it and danced away, opening it as she did.

"Let's see, my guess is we have two tickets to…"

She frowned. It wasn't tickets. It was her birth certificate—the original hospital copy—but it had another man's name on it name on it where Charlie's should have been.

"Daddy? I don't—what is this?"

Charlie sank onto the chair and put his head in his hands. Ten, her legs suddenly weak, sat across from him and waited.

"I never wanted you to know, sweetheart. It's all too—your life was already a circus, thanks to me. I thought if we kept this part quiet, you could grow up as close to normal as possible."

"*Normal* has never been in our vocabulary. You're *not* my father? Jesus. I feel like I'm on a Maury Povich or Jerry Springer show."

Ten had grown up believing that her mother— Tomi Lyn Shepherd—was someone he'd hooked up with once back in his wilder days. A nice girl, but troubled. They both moved on quickly and he never saw her again.

A year later, a lawyer showed up at the rink and said Tomi Lyn had died, leaving behind a child, who just happened to be Charlie's. He raised her ever since. At least, that'd been the story she'd grown up hearing.

The woman—Tomi Lyn—had no known family and all Ten had of her was a grainy photograph and a baby blanket. No memory of her flickered in Ten's mind and she felt no sense of loss for the mother she never knew. Besides, it served no purpose to dwell on something she couldn't change. Ten accepted it. But wrongly believing the man across from her was her father? That had the power to devastate her.

"Sweetheart, I *am* your father, one hundred percent."

"So, what are you not telling me then? Why is there another man's name listed as my father on my birth certificate?"

Charlie rubbed his cheeks up and down. "Ah, kid. I never wanted you to know the real story. You ain't gonna quit till I tell you, though, are you?"

Ten crossed her arms over her chest and shook her head.

Charlie told her about her mother as delicately as he could. She and Charlie had a brief fling; that must was true. Tomi Lynn had a bigger prize in her sights, though. Bobby 'The Hammer' Harris. He was the face back then, and the better ticket. Happened all the time.

"So, basically, my mother was a ring rat. Great."

Charlie tried to soften the blow. "No, honey. She had this... something about her—a mystique, or whatever—that made her stand out. She wasn't like the others."

He went on. Ten read between the lines and gathered no one knew her story—at least not her *real* story, since she told many versions of it—and in the eighties, no one really cared.

"So, we parted ways. I wished her well. No hard feelings, you know? She followed Bobby to the east coast, I went west for a while. I didn't think much of it. My career was taking off."

A few months down the road Charlie ran into her after a show. She'd changed in those few months, and not for the better. He asked how she was, and she told him she was pregnant with Bobby's kid.

"I point blank asked her if it—sorry— *you* were mine. She said no way."

To Ten, it was obvious she wanted to ride the coattails of the more famous wrestler. Her father was just too kind to say it.

"Gold-digger," said Kablooey from the kitchen doorway. He'd let himself in and picked up the story. "That's what I told your pop. Told him, c'mon, man. We see it all the time. Let Bobby deal with her. Hurricane Harper was on his way to becoming the face. Everything played out just like I thought it would, too."

Ten looked from one to the other. "Meaning what?"

Charlie gave Kablooey a warning glance. "Sweetheart, your... mother wasn't a bad person. She just, I don't know, came up hard or something and that made her do some things she maybe wouldn't have otherwise. It was a wild time, you know?"

Kablooey snorted. "Oh, it was wild, all right. Bobby was juicin' hard—most everyone was—and then the coke, and the partying, and God knows what else. Hey, remember that time when—"

"Anyhow," said Charlie with another pointed look to Kablooey, "Bobby wasn't interested in having a kid. Tomi bet on the wrong horse and she lost. I don't know what happened between them or where she went when he kicked her out. All I knew was that she was gone."

Charlie grabbed a couple beers from the fridge as Kablooey picked up the story.

"Bout six months later, she knocked on his dressing room door. I was with him when she showed up. She had an infant in one of them baby carrier things and looked like hell. You were cute as a button, though."

"Thanks, Bloo."

"Sure thing, kid. Anyhow, she says to him, 'I lied, Charlie. She's yours. I can't take care of her,' and sets the carrier and a diaper bag down on the floor."

Charlie looked off into the distance, remembering. "Tomi said she had no money, no place to stay, no family. I offered to help her, put her up and give her cash. I figured, even if you weren't mine, I couldn't let you suffer. What kind of man would I be if I did that?"

He bowed his head and shook it slowly.

"Then I saw her arms. Full of track marks, Ten. I looked from her to you, and damn if you weren't smiling up at me. Man, I fell head over bootstraps in love with you right there. Before I even knew I was saying it, I told her I'd take you, but she had to go into rehab."

"Your pop foot the bill for that. Only this guy here gets his first big payday and spends it all on a—on a woman he hardly knows and takes on a kid he don't even know is his or not."

Charlie ignored him and said, "We did it all legal. Temporary guardianship at first. Then I had a paternity test done. As soon as I found out I was really your dad, we had the birth certificate changed. I don't know why the hell I kept the old one. It was stupid."

"Okay, so, you took me in. She went to rehab. Then where'd she go? Did she ever try to come back for me? Is she—"

"I told her if she got clean, she could come back, be a part of your life. But Tomi left rehab early and disappeared. That's when I filed for sole custody."

Tenley's tone was matter of fact. "She never came back."

"No, sweetheart. I-I've never seen or heard from her since."

She waited to see if anger or sadness, or some other normal reaction to shocking news would overcome her. There was nothing aside from wonder. Then a thought came to her.

"She's still alive, isn't she?"

Charlie and Kablooey exchanged pained looks. Ten read between the lines. She didn't wait for the answer.

She asked, "Did you tell any of this to Nick Keller?"

"Yes. All of it. Off the record, of course. He kept his promise, Ten. He never told a soul."

Her mind raced. He'd called her motherless. A wild child. What else had he written? It chagrined her to realize she didn't know. Ten stood.

"It's okay, Dad. Crazy as fuck, but okay. Don't worry, finding out my ring rat, druggie mother abandoned me to a pro-wrester she hardly knew has not scarred or traumatized me in any way. Do you still have a copy of the book?"

"My office, bookcase on the right, third shelf."

She was almost out the kitchen door before she abruptly went back to give her father a hug.

"Thanks for wanting me, Dad. I've loved every minute of our life together."

It was true. She wouldn't trade her unconventional life for anything, not even for having a mother. Charlie and her wrestling family had given her everything a girl could want. Love, attention, affection, killer moves in the ring, a strong backbone, and so much more.

Ten never remembered wanting for a mother. She supposed that was weird, but it was true. Charlie could twist a French braid as well as any mom. The birds and bees talk and the becoming a woman discussion were awkward but they both survived. She cried on his shoulder over boys, dragged him to the mall, and made him listen to Backstreet Boys on repeat. So, what did she need a mother for? Nothing, that's what. Nothing at all. Especially one who didn't even care enough to come back for her.

Ten blinked away the tears that obscured the book titles on the bookshelf. The red spine of _Eye of the Hurricane, The Life and Legacy of Charlie 'The Hurricane' Harper_ jumped out at her and she flipped to chapter four, titled, Charlie's Little Hurricane.

Skipping the part she knew, she read on for the first time since the book came out.

Though the news of Charlie Harper having an infant without a wife or partner leaked and raised many eyebrows, we know little of the circumstances. Charlie Harper has been adamant and vigilant in protecting his only daughter's privacy.

Many rumors abounded in the eighties about the child, Tenley Rose. The tabloids made many suppositions as to the parentage of the girl. Some said she was the love child of a former flame; others claimed a groupie left the child on his doorstep. Even more outlandish claims were made, all which Harper never acknowledged. When pressed for information about the child's mother, The Hurricane deadpanned his signature phrase. "You wanna get inside the eye of the Hurricane? You can come in, but you won't get out."

Ten had known of the old rumors, but Charlie had always fluffed them off as tabloid sensationalism and part of the territory of growing up famous. As for Nick Keller, he'd only written what was public knowledge and had furthermore hidden the truth out of respect for Charlie... and to protect Ten.

How could she have been so wrong about him? Then she remembered the other night on the beach. She pushed him away just like she pushed everyone away. Reject them before they could reject her. Maybe, somewhere in her DNA, she knew her own mother had left her and that was why she kept the world at bay?

Ten snorted at her own melodrama and flipped the book over to read the back. Who was she trying to fool? She wanted to see Nick's picture, the one she'd drawn devil horns and buck teeth on in permanent marker when it arrived in the mail.

"Oh, Keller. Who's the bad guy now, hmm? Guess I'd better try and fix this. But how?"

The party.

Ten whipped out her phone and opened the ongoing text messages with Margot.

Hey. Need a favor. Get an invite to Nick Keller for the party. Don't tell him it's from me. Say it's from my dad. Don't ask.

She had no idea what she'd say when she saw him. *If* she saw him. But she suspected he couldn't turn down his idol, even if it meant seeing Ten. She held her breath and hit 'send.'

[19] CHARLIE

Charlie and Kablooey stayed rooted to their chairs at the kitchen table. Shell-shocked. They didn't speak for a while, just listened to the sound of Tenley's footsteps fade down the hall. He thought he heard her sniff, like she was crying. He stood—started to, that is—but Kablooey shook his head. Then the office door closed.

"Shit," said Charlie.

"Shit," agreed Kablooey.

They drank their beers, then another.

"Did I do wrong by her?"

"Nah, man. You did right. She said so herself. You heard her."

"I mean, leavin' out the rest? That we know where Tomi Lyn is? The money?"

Kablooey set his beer bottle on the table and leaned his considerable weight forward.

"Listen, brother. Remember when I told you— back when you set up that fake corporation so you could send Tomi Lyn money for her dog rescue thing—that I wished Ten did know? It was only because I thought she should see what a selfless, good-hearted dude her pop was."

"Ah, stop. It was just something that I felt—"

"Like you had to do. I know, I was there, tryin' to talk you out of it, remember? You said, '*No matter what Tomi Lyn is or isn't, she's still the mother of my child.*' I never forgot that, man."

Kablooey shook his head, smiling.

"I thought, man, I wish Tenley knew just how great her dad really is. Then today, I see her getting hit with this big fucking news, and instead of losing her shit, she pulls out the old Charlie Harper logic." He laughed. "So, to answer your question? You did *right*, my friend."

Kablooey stood, let out a belch, and said, "All right. Enough of this mushy crap. I'm outta here. See ya later, Harper."

"See you, Bloo," said Charlie.

After Kablooey left, Charlie opened the box, still on the far end of the table, and reached around until his fingers brushed the hard edge of a polaroid. He lifted it out and studied the photograph. He wore his dark purple trunks and his W.C.A. World Champion belt slung over one massive shoulder.

Under the enormous wing of his other arm, a skinny brunette with bangs and big eyes lined in blue eyeliner smiled at the camera. Even though it was the eighties, she had the look of a hippie. Hair down to her waist, a few thin braids tied off with feathers and string at the end. She wore a tight top that showed most of her flat stomach and pants that sat low on her hips, below her navel. She looked like she'd stepped out of one time and into another.

He read the black marker inscription in the thick white space at the bottom. Hurricane + Tomi Lyn 1988. Tomi Lyn's handwriting, not his. Charlie never told Kablooey—or anyone—he would've married Tomi Lyn. True, he didn't love her, and she didn't love him, but he would've done it, if it could give Ten the kind of life she deserved.

Maybe that's not the best way to have a family, but he would've made it work for his little girl. He would've if she would've. But that's now how it went.

A long time passed before he accepted that Tomi Lyn wasn't coming back. He had his people track her down. It wasn't hard. What he'd learned made him relieved he didn't marry her, but it didn't make him happy.

She may have brought a shitty life onto herself, but that didn't mean she *deserved* it. Charlie knew plenty of good people in his lifetime that had gotten mixed up in the wrong shit. Didn't make them bad. It just made their choices bad. It could've been his path, too.

There was a quote he heard once from a wrestling buddy who'd turned religious. *There but for the grace of God go I*. Man, did that stick with him. He was *so close* to going down that wrong path. Closer than even Kablooey knew. Then, this little pink bundle of drool and Johnson's baby shampoo comes into his life and *bam*.

"There but for the grace of God go I," said Charlie to the photograph.

He debated whether to keep it out for Ten. Even set it on the table where she'd see it. He'd gone as far as her bedroom before he turned back to get it.

Not to hide, but to put away until the time was better, less raw. His girl had enough dropped on her in one day.

20 NICK

"Bro, you want to plant your feet in line with your shoulders and don't lock your elbows."

Nick looked at the younger, better built guy and almost told him to go fuck himself. Then he recognized him. Ten's boy-toy. What the hell was his name again? Jason? Jimmy?

"I'm Josh. Personal trainer. Sorry, can't help myself sometimes."

Josh. That's right.

"Nah, it's cool. 'preciate it. Name's Nick."

Since he had two dumbbells in his grip, he jerked his chin in the universal, *hey, what's up* guy greeting.

"Nick Keller, right? You wrote that book about Charlie The Hurricane Harper?"

"Among others. You read it?"

"Some. I'm seeing his daughter. You know, Tenley? At least, I think I am."

The kid looked so dejected Nick found himself feeling bad for him. Not *too* bad, though.

Nick forced a neutral, vaguely sympathetic tone. "Trouble in paradise, I take it?"

Josh the boy-man shrugged then picked up his weights. Triple what Nick lifted, he noted.

"I don't know what's up with her, man. One minute everything's great. The next, I can't get her to answer my calls. She blew me off the other night, too."

Nick smirked, then covered it quickly with a frown. "That sucks, man. Ten's a complicated woman."

Josh looked at Nick with a new interest. The suspicious kind. "*Ten*, huh? Didn't realize you two were friendly. Last I knew she hated your guts."

"Ah, well—"

"Your book is in her dad's office, you know. She drew devil horns and, like, buck teeth on your picture."

"Of course, she did," muttered Nick. To Josh he said, "Like I said, complicated."

Josh's dead lifts became more aggressive and Nick took his cue to walk away before the boy-man dead lifted him. His phone buzzed in his pocket. He checked the text message and grinned.

"Nice meeting you, kid. Good luck with Ten...*ley.*"

"You, too, bro. Wait—I didn't mean good luck with Ten. I mean—"

"All good. See ya at the party."

"Yeah, sure. Wait, what part—"

Nick left with a satisfied smirk plastered on his face. It dropped when he walked into a brick wall named Kablooey.

"Keller. We need to talk."

Nick's mind raced. Had Harper told her father and surrogate uncle about the tumor? Or did she tell them Nick upset her and now he was here to rough him up. Was he seriously afraid of a seventy-year-old man? Yes. Yes, he was.

He forced a casual, "Hey, Bloo. What's up?"

"You talk to Ten lately?"

"I, uh, talk? I mean, like, not *talk* talk. But, you know, talk. Sure. But not..." he let the words drift off.

Kablooey squinted at him. "You on the drugs, Keller? Jesus. Ten found out about her mother the other night. She's been actin' weird ever since. Says she's fine, but…"

"Wow. How'd she take it?"

"Girl finds out her mother is a ring rat druggie who abandoned her to a wrestler she barely knew. How do you think she took it?"

"Whoa, sorry, man. Just—"

"Shit, no, I'm sorry. We're worried about her. If she talks to you, let her know we're here for her."

"Sure, will do. But Bloo? Why do you think she'd talk to *me* about it?"

Kablooey dismissed him with a wave of one beefy hand. "Oh, please. You two been circling each other for years. I figured something like this would finally bring you together or something. Plus, she knows that you know."

"Oh," said Nick. *Holy shit. She knows.* "Bloo, I gotta roll. Don't worry, if I see her, I'll tell her." He stopped. "Hey, is there—did she mention anything else? About herself, I mean?"

"What? No. Why?"

"Nothing, nothing. Never mind."

He knew where to find her. Poor Harper. Going through the worst time in her life, and he just walked away from her like it was nothing. Two days ago.

You're such a dick, Keller.

If memory served, she often went to the pier to paint whenever something upset her.

Bet the man-boy doesn't know that.

Petty jealousy was an unattractive trait, but damned if he could help himself when it came to that woman. He wanted to be the one by her side as she handled this brain tumor. Not some muscle-head kid, for fuck's sake. And that punk had nothing to do with Nick getting back into the gym. Nothing.

Nick climbed on his mountain bike—new, top of the line— and pedaled toward the pier. If he knew Harper at all, that's where he'd find her.

<u>21 KENNY</u>

Kenny pulled out of the teacher's lot for the last time of the school year. Principal Talbot had gone easy on him for his little disappearing act, less so regarding his arrest. The saving grace—and saving of his job—came when the charges dropped.

As for Lee, who'd not called or emailed either Kenny or the school in two weeks, her status remained uncertain. Elizabeth Talbot spoke with her usual monotonic pragmatism.

"Well, Kenneth. You've had quite the few weeks, haven't you? Given that we are at the end school year, and both you and Lee have been exemplary staff members—until as of late—I think we can postpone any disciplinary actions until the fall."

"Thank you, Eliz—"

"You will have your... personal situation resolved by then, I'm sure?"

"Oh, yes. I'm—"

"Excellent. We'll see you in July for orientation. Have a delightful summer, Kenneth. I... wish you and Lee the best."

Before Kenny could respond, Principal Talbot turned her attention to her computer, all but dismissing him. He murmured his thanks and slipped from her office, walk-running to his car in case she changed her mind. And because Fuchsia was waiting for him at Cappy's. First, he needed to stop home.

"Hey, Eddie," called Kenny over the hedges.

"Harper," said Eddie. Gone was the friendly tone.

Kenny supposed they were the talk of the neighborhood. News of Lee's abrupt departure and rumors of an impending divorce had come back to him by way of their mailman.

"I'll, uh, try and make next week's meeting, but I—"

"Sure thing. Will your... *wife* be attending?"

"Uh, maybe. I'll let you know."

Kenny dashed inside before his nosy neighbor could ask any more questions. He never realized before, but that guy was kind of an asshole.

"Hey, Dexter, old boy. Sorry I haven't been around much, buddy."

Kenny filled his food dish and refreshed the water bowl. Dexter sunned himself on the window ledge and awarded Kenny with a lazy glance before resuming an intense paw-licking regimen.

Upstairs in the bedroom that once held two people's belongings, Kenny changed into shorts and a t-shirt, tossing the work clothes onto the ever-increasing pile of dirty laundry.

In the kitchen he scrounged for something edible from the near bare refrigerator. Expired yogurt, wilted lettuce, a picked apart rotisserie chicken with whiskers, fruit salad that resembled soup. He'd eat at Cappy's. *If* he held onto his appetite.

Today was the day he would confront Lee. Fuchsia and all his new friends from the burlesque show finally convinced him that a reckoning was in order. Someone had to file for divorce if that's where they were heading.

"You're letting that woman walk all over you, babe," said Fuchsia.

"She left you high and dry, shacked up with another man, and you afraid to tell her you want some answers? Come on, now boy," said Scarlett O'Drama—aka Joey O'Hara.

Kitty Van Purr, also known as Daniel Stevens, concurred, adding, "Besides, Mr. Looks Like Gosling, you got a fine ass woman waiting in the wings. Why you wanna waste your time on some run-around Sue?"

Kenny had balked. "Who? No one is waiting in the wings for me."

Fuchsia palm-smacked his forehead. The others groaned.

"*Jacqui*, you fool. That girl has it *bad* for you, Gosling."

Kenny shook his head. "No, she wants nothing to do with me. Told me to have a nice life, see you around."

"That's maybe what she *said*, but it ain't what she *meant*. Trust me, lover boy. I know things."

Fuchsia's words echoed in his head as he snatched his keys off the counter and moved toward the door. The blinking light on the answering machine caught his eye. He almost ignored it, but then considered it might be Lee. He hit the play button.

"Hello, this is Dr. Kerns office calling for Tenley Harper. Could you please call us back right away? It's regarding your—there's been—well, call us back right away."

Kenny replayed the message, this time taking down the number the receptionist left at the end. In the car, he dialed the number. The same receptionist's voice came through the Bluetooth speakers.

"Dr. Ker—Dr. Rue's office, can I help you?"

"Ah, yes. Wait, this is Dr. Kerns office, right?"

The receptionist hedged. "Y-yes. Dr. Rue will be taking over Dr. Kerns patients. I'm afraid Dr. Kerns passed away unexpectedly two weeks ago."

"Oh," said Kenny. "I'm sorry to hear that. I know my wife was fond of him. That must be why we received a call from the office, to let her know."

A pause. "What is your wife's name, please?"

"Lee Harper. Well, Tenley Harper, technically."

"I see. Could you hold please?"

Kenny heard a click, then tinny Muzak filled the car. After an eternity, a man's voice came on the line.

"Mr. Harper? This is Dr. Rue. I'm afraid a mistake has been made. A rather serious one. I see you're authorized to receive information regarding your wife's health, so allow me to explain."

Kenny felt a knot form in his stomach. "That's correct. Go ahead."

"Two women with the same name—Tenley Harper—visited our office, on the same day. There's no easy way to say this," the doctor paused, cleared his throat, "the test results were confused. That is, they received each other's results, and not their own. We're terribly sorry for the mix up. One in a million odds. Two Tenleys."

"Two Tenleys," echoed Kenny.

"Ah, yes. Mr. Harper. We need to see your wife as soon as possible to discuss options. A brain tumor is obviously quite serious. We've been trying to reach her, but her inbox is full.

"Options. You mean treatment options?"

Another pause. "Mr. Harper. Your wife's tumor is inoperable. We need to discuss hospice care."

"I-I see. Yes, of course." Kenny swallowed hard. "We'll be in touch, Dr... I'm sorry your name again?"

"Rue. Dr. Keaton Rue. My direct number is—"

Kenny disconnected the call. He didn't need Dr. Rue's direct line. He needed to find his wife.

²² TEN

Ten pulled her phone from her tote. Six messages. She sighed and hit play.

"Hey sweetie. It's Margot. Listen, would it be weird if your dad and I came to Cappy's tonight? You know, together? He said he told you about us. Crazy, huh? I mean, who'd have thought, after all this time. Guess it's what they say— chemistry and timing. Anyhow, call me back. And do not blow us off again. Oh, and your hunk came looking for you. Twice, FYI."

The next message came from her father. "Sweetheart, it's your dad. Guess you know that already, though. Listen, Margot and I are coming to Cappy's tonight. Just wanna make sure that's kosher. Call me."

A third, fourth, and fifth all from Josh. Same message. "Ten. It's Josh. Call me back, please."

The fifth was from a number she didn't recognize, and so didn't bother to play it. What did it matter if someone wanted to sell her a new warrantee on her car? Or offer her a lifetime magazine subscription? She'd be dead in a matter of months.

She set up her easel and clamped on a canvas, pulled out her paints and brushes and two bottles of water. One for drinking, one for the brushes. Painting always soothed Ten's soul, but today her thoughts were dark and morbid, and the first bold strokes of black revealed it.

How will it happen?

Would she go to sleep on night and never wake up? Would she lose her ability to function, to speak or see? What if she spent her last days trapped inside her body, like a vegetable, but aware and unable to respond? Should she end her own life before the tumor rendered her incapacitated?

End my own life.

Such a thought never entered Ten's mind before. She *loved* her life. So much so, that she had no bitterness or resentment for her mother.

Besides, what kind of life might Ten have had if Tomi Lynn Shepherd kept her?

Then I saw her arms. Full of track marks.

A shudder rippled through Ten's body. At least the woman gave enough of a shit to give her up instead of dragging her through hell. The name for the emotion she felt came to Ten as she grabbed a new brush, dipped in the white. Grateful.

White streaked through the black. She added more in long, sweeping strokes. The sea danced below and stretched out wide before her, constant waves undulating in the fading sunlight. If she sat still, keeping the ocean in her peripheral vision, it felt like being on a boat, like she moved through the water. The illusion enchanted her as a child, and still did as a woman.

A smile lit her face. Ten's true nature made it impossible not to feel joy in this heaven on earth. A place she'd lived her whole life… and would meet her death in. It was too damn soon, and she wasn't ready but if that's what the universe wanted for her, then…

"So be it."

"Talking to yourself, now, Harper?"

Nick.

She should've been surprised, yet she felt none. "Hello again, Keller. Fancy seeing you out here."

Their smiles were shy, cautious. Whatever harshness there was between them two nights ago seemed forgiven and forgotten by both. Ten swiped the last paint strokes on the canvas. Nick stood close behind her.

"What do you think, Keller?"

She studied his face as his eyes scanned the painting, trying to memorize every detail. The fine lines at the corners of his eyes. The flecks of gold in his irises. His slightly crooked nose. The sharp line of his jaw, the jagged, raised scar on the underside of his chin. His throat, collarbone.

"I think…" his voice caught. "I think you're the love of my life Harper. I know that sounds corny, but—"

"I love you, too, Keller."

Her paintbrush clattered to the floorboards. His hands against her damp cheeks, fingers twined through her hair. The kiss—five years in the waiting—was like no other before. It was a kiss to die for.

Ten smiled against his lips. He pulled back just a little.

"You're thinking morbid thoughts, aren't you, Harper?"

"How'd you know?"

"I've met you, remember?" He tilted his head at the canvas. "Plus, the angel wings dipped in black is a bit of a tip off."

Ten looked at the painting and laughed through her nose. "I didn't even realize what I painted. It *is* kind of twisted, isn't it?"

"You think? Most people who paint on the beach try and capture the sunset or dolphins swimming. Not you, kid."

"Oh, shut up and help me pack this stuff up."

They gently teased and chided each other on the walk back to the house. As they got closer, their steps slowed, and the banter dropped off.

"I'm not ready to give you up, Harper. I've waited too long."

"Inoperable, Nick. I don't think we have a choice here."

"I don't care. We'll find another doctor. A specialist. Alternative medicine. Pot. Anything is better than nothing."

"Nick, I looked it up. Glioblastomas. They're almost impossible to treat."

"Ha! *Almost* impossible, but not impossible. Come on, Ten. You've got to fight this. Jesus, how are you so—so *accepting*?"

"Because... because of the words, Keller. Inoperable. Terminal. All I can do is choose to go with dignity and grace."

They took a few more steps. Ten's tone softened. "We'll see. No promises, Nick. If it's my turn, I want to go on my own terms. As much as possible, anyway. No chemo, or radiation, no experimental drugs. Not if the odds are too high against it working."

"It because you volunteered in that hospice, isn't it?"

Ten was taken aback. "You knew about that? I never told anyone I went there."

Nick looked down. "My mother was there for a few months. I saw you walk by every week."

"Oh, Nick..."

"It's okay. I mean, it was fucking awful. But—" He stopped, understanding dawning across his face. "That's why you're not trying to fight, isn't't? You saw what it was like for them, for the families, too."

There was nothing to add, Nick understood her motivation even before she had. As soon as he said the words, she nodded. It was just how she felt.

"I'm not giving up, Nick. I'm just giving in."

"That might be semantics, Harper, but I get it."

They reached the house and stood outside the gate, watching the hustle and bustle of the event planning staff as they set tables up, flipped open folding chairs, popped canopies open, and rolled portable tiki bars to opposite ends of the pool.

"Jesus, Harper. How many people you have coming to this thing?"

"About a hundred."

Nick grinned at Tenley and she shrugged.

"Go big or go home, huh?"

Neither spoke a word about last hurrahs nor going out with a bang.

"Come on in and say hi to my dad."

"To your dad? You sure? I mean—"

"Keller, we don't hate each other anymore, don't be stupid."

"For the record, I never hated *you*."

Ten gave him a playful shove. "Aww, so romantic."

"It's just the beginning, Harper."

"Well, technically, it's—"

"Don't do it. Do not ruin this charming banter with a morbid comment."

Ten rolled her eyes. "Humor is the best medicine. God, everyone knows that."

She took Nick's hand and pulled him inside the house. Her phone buzzed in her pocket. It was the same unfamiliar number as before. *Later.* Whoever it was could wait.

²³ <u>NICK</u>

Nick remained straddled between cloud nine and a nightmare. The woman he loved said she loved him back. That same woman was dying from an inoperable brain tumor. What were the odds on that? And while he was at it, how bizarre was it he was on an errand to buy fresh flower leis for Hurricane Harper's luau themed birthday party *while* those facts swirled in his head?

He always knew getting involved with Tenley Harper meant being sucked into a crazy vortex world where up was down, but he hadn't ever envisioned anything like this. Yet, he had no desire to walk away. It surprised no one more than Nick Keller. Hell, if someone had told him a month ago that he'd knowingly get involved with a woman who was dying, he'd have said they were nuts. If they'd told him it was with *Tenley Harper*, he'd have had them committed on grounds of said insanity.

But here they were, holding hands and walking into Livvy's Flower Shop as if all was right in the world. Nick checked his phone while Ten spoke with the florist. Missed call from a Connecticut number. His heart thumped hard against his chest.

"Harper, just going to make a call outside, okay?"

"Sure, we'll be a few minutes anyhow. You okay? You look... I don't know, weird."

"What? Yeah, no. Fine, I'm fine. Be right back."

He wasn't fine. He did a thing, a potentially stupid thing and there was a high likelihood that Harper would be pissed about it. Still, he started it, so he had to see it through.

"Hello?"

"Uh, hi. I'm returning your call. This is Nick Keller."

"Oh, right. Yeah. Your message yesterday said you're interested in one of my rescue dogs? Your area code is Florida. That's a long way to travel for a dog, isn't it?"

Nick took a deep breath. "I saw on your website that the woman who runs the rescue is named Tomi Lynn. Would it be possible to speak to her?"

There was a long pause. "This is she. Tomi Lynn Wakefield. How can I help you?"

Sweat prickled in his armpits. "Did your last name used to be Shepherd?"

Another pause, longer this time. "Who wants to know?"

"Mrs. Wakefield, did you have a child—a girl—thirty-six years ago?"

"Listen, I don't know what—"

"Her name is Tenley Rose Harper. She knows all about the circumstances of your—of her—well, she knows about you. I think it might be good for you both to meet."

"That so? Then why are *you* calling, and not her?"

"So, you *are* Tomi Lynn Shepherd?"

"Yes."

Nick heard the tremor in her voice and softened his tone. "She's an amazing woman, Mrs. Wakefield. Can I fly you down here to meet her?"

"I—y-yes. Are you sure she wants to meet me? She must hate me…"

"I can assure you she doesn't hate you."

"You haven't told her you found me, have you?"

"Not exactly, ma'am. But don't worry, I'll take care of everything. You just get to Bradley Airport tomorrow afternoon. I got you a direct flight into Tampa. I'll email you your confirmation code."

"Tomorrow? Jesus. You already bought a ticket? You in some kind of hurry? How'd you know I'd say yes?"

"I didn't. And yes, I am in a hurry. Time is—well, time is moving quickly."

"Is there something you're not telling me, Mr. Keller? She's not—there's nothing wrong with her, is there?"

Telling the woman that her daughter has an inoperable brain tumor wasn't something you said over the phone.

"Everything's fine, Mrs. Wakefield."

"All right then. Guess I'll be seeing you tomorrow."

Just as Nick ended the call, Ten came out of the store with a long cardboard box overflowing with floral leis.

Her smile was warm and without suspicion. "Done with your call?"

"Yup, all done," said Nick.

"Great. Take these and put them in the backseat, will you?"

"Sure thing."

She stared at him anew, a puzzled expression on her face, "You sure you're okay? Anything you need to tell me? I hope you're not up to any tricks or planning any surprises, Keller. You know I hate surprises, right?"

"*Pshht*. Nah. Don't be silly, Harper." Nick's laugh sounded forced and nervous even to his own ears. "Come on, let's get these to your place before they wilt in this heat."

He ignored her continued stare and climbed into the convertible's passenger seat. Internally, he swore and stressed. Externally, he tried to appear cheerful and carefree., Harper was too busy discussing party arrangements to grill him any further.

What have you done, Keller? She'll kill you for this.

He had to confess his impulsive, possibly idiotic idea to someone. By right, it should be to Harper. That was the only logical conclusion.

"Harper? Could you drop me off at the gym?"

She glanced at him. "The gym? You want me to drop you off at the gym? Now?"

"Mhm."

"You're wearing sandals, Keller."

"What? Oh, right. Yeah, no I have gym clothes there. I-it won't take long. I'll meet you at your place in an hour, okay?"

Ten shrugged. "Suit yourself, Keller."

Five minutes later he faced Louie Kablooey across an office desk. The big Samoan cracked open another pistachio shell from the giant bowl in front of him.

"You want some pistachios?" He pronounced it *pi-ta-chios.*

"Ah, no thanks."

"They're good. Have some pistachios."

When a three-hundred-and-seventy-five-pound Samoan tells you to have some pistachios, you have them. They cracked shells and ate in awkward silence. Awkward to Nick, at least. Kablooey seemed perfectly content.

"So, I wanted to talk to you about Ten."

"I figured. You do something stupid?"

"I—why would you—yes." Nick sank back against the chair.

"Spill it."

There was no skirting it. "I found her mother."

"That all? You want a medal? She's not hard to find, Keller."

Nick blinked at the big man. "You guys knew where she was this whole time?"

Kablooey shrugged. "Charlie been sending her money for twenty years. Helped her set up that dog rescue of hers."

Nick's heart sank. "Oh, fuck. She's black-mailing him?"

"Nah, nothing like that. Geez, you been watching too much soap operas, Keller. He sends it anonymously, through a foundation."

"And Ten doesn't know?"

"Of course not, dummy. Tomi cleaned up almost thirty years ago and never came for her kid. Never called. Never tried to find out about her. Nothing. Why would we tell her any of that?"

Nick processed the new information with dread. "So, you—Charlie—never reached out to her? Or, like try to reunite them?"

"Only an idiot would try to put them together. Tell me you're not an idiot, Keller."

Nick dropped his head in his hands. "I'm an idiot, Bloo."

24 LEE

Lee walked into the brightly lit gym, her bag slung over her shoulder and water bottle in hand. Along one side of the long, rectangular room ran a mirrored wall. Men and women with bulging muscles and outfits that left nothing to the imagination lifted free weights, grimacing and watching their form.

Opposite, a bank of black and ruby-red exercise machines lined the floor like ground force soldiers awaiting orders to charge. Treadmills, stationary bikes, and ellipticals in the same color scheme held the front line, and an array of equipment cued up behind them. More than half were in use.

There were no televisions mounted to the walls like at her gym back home, no motivational quotes stenciled onto the walls, and no discouragement for lifting hard and heavy. Instead, loud, aggressive music played from the speakers and over that, the guttural grunts and loud metallic clanks of people dead serious about their workouts.

Lee tucked her hair behind her ear and looked around for her trainer. She'd only seen a picture of him, but she'd been confident she'd recognize him. Looking at all the muscle-bound young men, she began to doubt her assertion.

"Lee? Hi, sorry. Are you Lee?"

A ridiculously good-looking young man with a movie star smile and Superman physique strode over to her, hand extended. She took it and nodded. Her cheeks burned and she regretted not wearing any makeup. Then Lee reminded herself that those neurotic thoughts belonged to old Lee, not new Lee.

"Hi, you must be Josh. Nice to finally meet you in person."

"Yeah, totally." He appraised her with the eye of a professional. "You've got, like, a natural, athletic build. You a runner?"

She nodded.

"Yup, shows. Long, lean muscles. We need to up your calories, though. Little too lean. Any physical limitations I need to be aware of?"

"Nope. Healthy as a horse," said Lee.

"Great. Just gonna have you fill out this form. Medical history and contact info, the usual. Soon as you're done, we'll get started."

Josh sat her at a small table on the business side of the gym. Lee filled out the form, then waited for Josh to come back. Across from her was an office with the shade open. She couldn't help but look in. A large, roundish man sat behind a desk, facing Lee and popping what looked like pistachios in his mouth, while another man—his back to Lee—gestured and bobbed his head.

When they stood and moved toward the door, she dropped her head back to the paperwork as if she hadn't been trying to decipher their conversation.

"Well, kid, all I know is you better fix this, quick. I'd still like to know why you pulled such a rookie stunt like that."

"I know, I know. I'll figure something out."

"Miss? Is anyone helping you," asked the big man.

Lee looked up, "Oh, yes, thanks. I'm here for—
"

"She's with me, boss," said Josh, coming around the corner.

"Hey, I know you," said the third man.

Lee turned to him and remembered, "Ah, yes. You're the guy from the street. With the angry girlfriend."

"You're the jaywalker. Oh, and she wasn't my girlfriend."

Lee caught the nervous glance he shot the round man and Josh. Before she could say anything, the man Josh called boss pulled him into his office.

"One more sec, Lee, and we'll get started on a workout."

When the two were out of earshot, Lee said, "Sorry about that. Let me guess. You're involved with that guy's daughter?"

"What? No. Close but no cigar. I'm involved with his niece. But I wasn't when you and I crossed paths. For the record."

"Sure." Lee shrugged but her smirk said she didn't buy it.

"Seriously. I wasn't. I'm Nick."

"Hello, Nick. I'm Lee."

"Say, you're not the one dating my buddy Max, are you?"

She laughed. "Word gets around in a small town, huh?"

"Shit, yeah. So, I'll see you at the party tonight, then?"

Lee blinked in surprise. "You're going to the party?"

"Yup. Kablooey's niece is my girl. Her name is—"

"What did you just say, Keller?"

Easy-going, good-natured Josh now looked anything but friendly. He looked ready to charge the taller, much less muscular man.

Lee, a beat behind, said, "I'm sorry, did you say… Kablooey? Who is—"

The big man stepped between the two younger ones. "That'd be me, Miss. Louis Tamatoa, at your service. Josh here will take you around the gym, show you the equipment." He turned to Nick and said, "And you're just leaving, right?"

Nick saluted the man with the silly name, tipped an imaginary cap to Lee, and smiled as he sauntered past Josh. Both Lee and Kablooey rolled their eyes at the testosterone show.

"It's very nice to meet you, Mr. Kablooey—ah, Tamatoa. I'm Lee."

"It's just Kablooey, sweetheart. Wait, did you say Lee? As in Max's Lee?"

Did the *whole* town know about her? The idea made her feel warm inside. She'd never belonged anywhere before, and now these people, these strangers, accepted her with open arms. Literally. Kablooey had wrapped his beefy arms around her and said something that sounded like, 'Sue Sue My.'

"It means welcome," said Kablooey. To Josh, he said, "You cool off yet, Romeo?"

"Yes, sir," said Josh.

"Good. Get back to work."

Josh, with admirable effort to rally, brought Lee around the whole gym, showing her how to use each machine. At the end, they decided on a workout schedule and said their goodbyes.

"Hey, before you go, can I ask you something?"

"Sure," said Lee.

"All right, it's, like, a scenario, okay? Like, say you were dating one guy—he's like, a *really* great guy who'd do anything for you—but then another guy kinda swoops in and, I don't know, distracts you or something. Would you want the first guy—the good one—to try and win you back?"

Lee breathed in slowly and considered her response. Her thoughts jumped between Max and Kenny. Would she want Kenny to confront Max or fight for her? The answer was simple. *No.*

Lee never was that girl who tried to make a boyfriend jealous just to have proof of their love. The men she dated weren't fighters, anyhow. Or lovers, really. They were the middle of the road guys. Not quite the brainiacs, not the jocks. They were the guys you had to look back through old yearbooks to find, so you could put a name to a face.

Rachel with the navel piercing once suggested that she dated below her level of attractiveness because she liked to have all the power. Lee had scoffed at that, half flattered and half feeling bad for Kenny. He *was* a good-looking guy. He just wasn't stylish. Or cool. Or self-aware. Poor Kenny. In the quiet of her own mind, Lee confessed a buried truth. She'd stopped loving him a long time ago.

Josh the man-boy stared expectantly at her, bringing Lee back to present. As much as she wanted to say, 'Let her go, sweetie,' she had to remember her situation didn't mirror Josh's situation. Plus, he looked at her like a hopeful puppy.

"I think, Josh, you have to do whatever your instincts tell you to do. What's meant to be, will be."

Josh stared off into the distance for a moment, bobbed his head, and said, "You know what, you're right. I'm gonna crash that party tonight and tell her how I feel. Thanks, Lee."

"Wait, I—"

It was too late. Josh had sprinted off toward the locker rooms. Lee stared after him, uncertain. On one hand, she was sorry for the guy, and wanted to stop him from humiliating himself. But that again led her to feeling bad for Kenny and imagining him doing something so mortifying. Guilt, sudden and sharp stabbed through the cracks in her armor. She didn't want to feel guilty.

"Stop it, damn it."

A few of the gym patrons turned to look at her. Lee's headache returned with a vengeance and she hurried out, fumbling in her bag for the ibuprofen. Next door to the gym was a small coffee shop with bistro seating outside. On shaky legs she walked through the little wrought iron gate and sat down at the first table.

"Could I get a glass of water, please?"

The waitress brought water and a menu and asked if she was all right.

"Fine, thank you. I-I'll just have a croissant."

She didn't want the croissant, nor was she fine. She'd done terrible thing, leaving Kenny the way she had. He'd been a good, kind husband. Never cheated or lied. He worked hard and did the best he could. How could she have been so heartless?

Her thoughts of Kenny in these weeks were contempt filled and critical. She'd focused on everything he'd done wrong so she wouldn't have to think about the wrong she'd done. Anger was easier, it propelled her to act and sustained her righteousness.

But now the anger dissolved and dispersed like a rain cloud. The sun shone down and revealed two truths. Lee didn't love her kind, gentle husband anymore. But even so—especially so—he deserved better treatment.

Then there was her job. She walked away from her *job*, giving no notice. Sixteen years, down the drain. How would she make a living, if not through teaching?

Oh, my God, what have I done?

The avalanche continued. *Max.* Another good, sweet, kind man. He'd shown her nothing but a love so unguarded and unrestrained, and so undeserved by Lee. She'd repaid him with deceit from the moment they met.

Lee couldn't be sure, but she might be in love with him. Old Lee battled with New.

You can't be in love with a man you just met.

Yes, you can.

No, it's not plausible or practical.

Fuck plausible and practical. I've never been this happy.

Well too bad you blew it by lying to him.

Max's words come back to her.

The only thing worse than being an ax murderer is if you're married.

She was a married, jobless, adulteress liar. What was wrong with her? How had she drifted so far from who she thought she was? Could poor Kenny ever forgive her? Would Max ever speak to her again once he knew the truth? As if she'd conjured him, Max appeared.

"There you are," said Max. "I think I may have found the perfect place for—hey, what's wrong?"

Max hurried around the railing to her side.

"I'm fine, I—"

"Sweetheart, you're not fine, you're crying. What is it? Lee, whatever is going on with you, you can tell me. Don't you think it's time to let me in? That is, if you want this—us—to grow."

He knelt beside her chair and gazed up at her with such earnest worry and care. Lee took his warm, rough cheeks in her hands and kissed his mouth once, then again. In case it was the last time she have the chance to. She would tell him everything.

"Sit with me?"

He did, but only after pressing each of her palms to his lips. Her heart burned with the ache of losing him. She wasn't ready for such sweetness to end.

"Whatever it is, Lee, you can tell me. If its money you're worried about, you can stay with me for as long as you want. Honestly? I've grown quite fond of having you there."

Lee smiled through her tears. She'd begun searching for a place to live, despite those repeated offers from Max to stay with him. She needed to be on her own for a while, and not living with the first man she dated since… God, she couldn't yet say *divorced*, because she yet to even legally separate from Kenny. She'd just left.

She struggled to keep the sadness from her voice. "Thank you, Max. I've enjoyed it just as much. Too much, in fact."

Max paled. "Are you... are you breaking up with me?"

"No, not at all." She squeezed his hand. "I think once I... once you know—"

"Well, hey, if it isn't Pinellas County's favorite new couple. You two look like a travel guide photo."

It was Margot from Cappy's, followed by the same two that had been with her on the first day Lee came into the bar. Lucy and...

"Carlos, my God, get off your phone and say hello," said Lucy as she tapped on *her* phone.

Lee and Max exchanged glances then put on bright smiles and greeted the friends. In seconds, three metal chairs scraped across the patio to surround their table, and all spoke with animated gestures and theatric panache. Lee's relief at the interruption exacerbated her guilt, but she encouraged them.

Max's eyes drifted to her face, his expression puzzled and concerned. Lee mouthed, *'I'm fine'* and tried to keep pace with the rapid-fire banter. They jumped from outfits for the party to the potential hurricane off the coast, then back to their outfits.

"Lee, sweetie, you can meet us girls at my place to get ready, if you want."

"Oh, that's very—"

"I'm in the Palm Fiesta condominiums, just up the street from Max."

Max leaned in, "Oh, that's the place I started to tell you about, Lee. They have one for rent."

"They *had* one for rent. Sorry, babe, someone beat you to it," said Carlos. "My friend Vigo and his boyfriend Alexandro snatched it up this morning."

"Wait," said Margot, "You're looking for a place to rent? Oh, my God, I have the perfect place for you. My friend—the one who's throwing the party tonight—has a guest house and it just so happens to be empty right now. You'd be a perfect fit."

"That sounds amazing. Thank you, Margot."

"Ah, don't mention it. I'll put in the good word for you and it'll be as good as done. Welcome to the neighborhood, sweetie."

Despite everything, Lee grinned. Surely this was a sign that this was where she was meant to be? The misgivings and doubts sank below the surface again, and a new excitement for the future bubbled. Now, she just had to tell Max what her real story was. And file for divorce. And get a job. And... those worries weren't as far below the surface as she hoped.

25 KABLOOEY

"Swear to God, these people are gonna be the death of me."

"Bloo? Who you talkin' to?" Jade, his office manager, cocked her head at him.

Kablooey looked up from his paperwork at the dark-skinned beauty. He'd been accused of hiring a high number of stunning young women, to which he agreed happily. Beauty and brains, his favorite combination, he always replied.

"Myself, Amara. I'm the only one who'll listen."

"Oh, okay. You want me to play the world's smallest violin for you, or just leave you the reports?"

He scowled at her but Jade only laughed. She wasn't afraid of him. Hell, she wasn't afraid of anyone.

"Just the reports, wiseass."

"Whatever you say boss. Oh, I drove by the building—you know, the one on the corner of Melville? Anyhow, the For Lease sign is up. Thought you'd want to know."

"Thanks, kid."

Three years he'd been watching that property, waiting for it to go up for lease. It was a perfect spot for a second gym. One large enough for a standard ring for his wrestlers, boxers, and mixed martial arts. Now all he needed was a partner to go in on it.

He'd gone over to Charlie's to ask Mae, but shit was hitting the fan when he got there, so timing was off. No on could accuse Luis Tamatoa of being unperceptive. That's what Ten would've said if she knew Kablooey's thoughts right then.

Not that he made light of anything going on at the Harper house. Shit, he'd been a party to those secrets from the get-go. Encouraged it, too. He didn't want to say so to Charlie—he was hurtin' enough as it was—but he had his doubts about how they'd handled the Tomi Lyn situation.

Kablooey considered his own mother. The woman was a saint. Six boys that woman raised. Each one crazier than the last and she never complained. His father—God rest his soul—died just before Kablooey turned seventeen, leaving Atalia Tamatoa to raise them all on her own.

Kablooey smiled. Not completely on her own. Their community was strong and believed that it takes a village. He had many uncles—real and honorary—that reinforced and further instilled his father's values and beliefs. He'd been blessed with role models. They made him the man he was.

That's why he stepped up when Ten came into Charlie's life. Because it's what you do. Period. And when Hurricane got that the news he had Parkinson's he did again and for the same reason. Plus, the Harpers were his family. He loved Charlie like a brother and Ten like a daughter.

It hurt him to the bone to see that kid upset. Knowing her mother gave her up and walked away. Charlie, if he wanted to, could be all understanding and compassionate, but Kablooey couldn't do it. Couldn't bring himself to be okay with someone like that. Best he could do is let that sleeping dog lie, so to speak, and hope it stayed asleep for Ten's sake.

If that dumb fuck Nick Keller did what Kablooey thought he did—reach out to that poor excuse of a woman—he'd snap his neck. He meant what he'd said to him. Only an idiot would try to make that match happen. No way *that* heel would become a face. Unless… Shit, maybe he was getting soft in his old age.

He wasn't ever, not in a million years, think better of Tomi Lyn Shepherd but if Ten wanted her in her life—if she could forgive her—then Kablooey guessed he'd have to tolerate the woman. *If* a meeting ever happened. Maybe when Keller talks to her she'll chicken out. But if she doesn't chicken out…

"Then what?"

Kablooey opened the bottom drawer of his desk and pulled out an envelope from under the stack of files. Scrawled across the front in his own handwriting, the name Shepherd. He slipped out the yellowed, frayed slip of paper. The phone number—written in pencil—was barely legible and Kablooey needed his cheaters to read it. He picked up the phone and dialed. When the recorded memo ended and the beep came, he left his message.

"Yeah, it's Bloo. Guy named Nick Keller either has or will be calling looking for you. It's about your... it's about Ten. It's fine, if you wanna. Better if you don't, if ya ask me, but it ain't up to me, is it?"

Kablooey's chest expanded, then he breathed out into the receiver.

"I'm just sayin'... if you aint got your shit together, it'd be best if you stayed away. Otherwise, well, maybe it would do her good to get some, I don't know, closure or whatever."

He wanted to end it on a nicer note, but the best he could muster was, "Okay, then. Maybe we'll see you, then," before he slammed the phone back on the holder.

26 TEN

Ten stood before the full-length mirror, her head tilted. She'd chosen a form-fitting white maxi dress and paired it with a simple shell necklace and matching earrings. Her hair hung in loose, beach-tousled waves down her back, a magenta hibiscus flower tucked behind her ear.

"I look surprisingly normal for someone who's about to keel over, huh?"

Nick stood in the bedroom doorway. "You look like a goddess, Harper." He crossed the room and stood behind her, placing a kiss on her bare shoulder. "How are you feeling?"

"Nervous. I don't know why. I've thrown hundreds of parties over the years."

She tried to laugh it off, but Nick's expression was too solemn. They both knew from where her nerves stemmed. Ten made him promise they wouldn't speak of her illness that night, not to each other or to anyone else. This night was for her father, and it would be a night to remember.

"Guests are arriving. By the way, I just got put in a headlock by *the* Nicholai 'Russian Roulette' Petrov."

"And yet you're smiling?"

"Are you kidding? That might have been the highlight of my life. After convincing you to give me a chance, that is."

Ten rolled her eyes. "My stock will go down quite a bit tonight. The entire 1987 Dream Team is coming to surprise my father."

Nick stepped back, his jaw hanging. Ten could easily see the twelve-year-old boy in him shine through.

"The whole team? Bobby the Brain? The Volcano? Mr. Amazing? The—"

"All of them, yes. Can you keep it together, Keller? I can't have you embarrassing me out there, you know."

Nick sputtered. "I-yeah, sure. *Pshh*, no big deal. Just, you know, the greatest pro-wrestlers of all time in one place. Whatevs, yo."

"Did you just say *whatevs*? Oh, my God, Keller. I can't even. Focus, please. Are Max and his girlfriend here yet? What about Margot and the gang? Did the caterers—"

"Whoa, hey. Slow down. Yes, Max and his girlfriend are here and setting up. Margot and the merry band of misfits have yet to arrive, and the caterers are doing their job. Oh, and your DJ for after Max does his thing is here, too. See, all under control."

Ten exhaled. "Okay. Good. That's good."

"There is one thing. A small thing in the grand scheme of things."

"Let me guess. You want me to introduce you to the Dream Team. Fine, Keller. I will."

"No, it's not that. I mean, yes, I'd love that, but—"

"It's my father, isn't it? Is he not wearing the shirt I picked out for him? I knew it. He's wearing that damn shirt, Nick. Even if I have to force him. Come on."

"Harper, wait. I—"

"Hurry up, Keller."

No time to listen to Nick's fanboy prattling. She had the mother of all parties to throw. Out at the pool deck, she scanned the small but growing crowd. A group of cigar smoking, barrel-chested men in prerequisite Hawaiian shirts drank beer and guffawed in one corner. Another group of guests were already in the pool, umbrella adorned drinks held high. More wandered about.

At last, she spotted her father. He stood in the middle of five back-slapping, high-fiving fellow former wrestlers from his golden days and wore the shirt she'd picked out for him.

Satisfied, Ten turned her attention to the rest of the scene. Guests were filtering in from beachside and driveway, bowing their heads to receive their leis from the hired greeters. Everywhere she turned, smiling faces. It was all just how she'd envisioned it.

"See, all is well, Harper."

Nick grinned down at her. She moved closer to him, allowed his gravitational pull to draw her in. His arm slipped around her waist.

"Yes, it is, Keller." She tipped her head to meet his gaze. "But for how long?"

Instead of answering, Nick kissed the tip of her nose then pointed at Max. "This is for you, Harper."

Max played Can't Help Falling in Love on a keyboard. Nick pulled Ten into his arms and danced her to the makeshift dance floor. She gazed at him in disbelief.

"How did you know this was my favorite song, Keller?"

"I didn't. I knew it was *my* favorite and summed up how I feel about you."

"*Are* we fools, do you think?"

"Maybe, Harper. But I don't care. How about you?"

"Nah. Fuck it, let's be fools, then."

A female voice mingled with Max's. Ten craned her neck to see the mystery woman she'd heard so much—and yet so little—about. She had pale blonde hair that just barely brushed her bare shoulders in a razor-neat bob. A black, halter-style dress hugged her slight figure, reminding Ten of something out of an old black and white movie. She looked at the woman's face again. Something about it...

"I think I know her," said Ten.

"Who? Max's girlfriend? How do you know her?"

"I-I'm not sure. She looks familiar, though."

As Ten stared, the petite blonde's gaze met hers. They squinted and tilted their heads at one another, then recognition lit both their faces.

"Oh," said Ten.

"What? You figure out where you know her from?"

"She was there—at the doctor's office—when I got my diagnosis. In the waiting room. I think she was preparing for bad news, too."

"No shit? Small world," said Nick.

The song ended and Nick went to get drinks from the bar. Ten wanted to chat with the woman, but their set had just begun. Instead, she made the rounds and checked on her father.

"Are you having fun, Daddy?"

"Sweetheart, this is the best party ever. I can't believe how many of my old crew showed up. Makes an old man feel—" he coughed back the tremor in his voice, "well, it makes an old man feel damn good, kid."

"You deserve it, old man. Where's Mar—"

"Here I am, sunshine," sang Margot, teetering on high heels and sloshing the contents of the two drinks she carried over.

They air-kissed and Margot gave her the once over. "You are looking especially stunning, Miss Thing. Does that have anything to do with a certain author, maybe?"

"I take it everyone knows?"

"What? That you two are an item now? Of course."

Charlie added, "I heard from Kablooey that Josh knows, too."

Ten winced. She never ended up talking to him. But it had been a casual thing. No way it could upset him. She said as much.

"Not according to Bloo, kid. Said he was pretty bent out of shape. Thought he might even cry."

"Oh, stop it, Daddy. Don't exaggerate."

Charlie shrugged. "I'm just repeatin' what Kablooey told me."

He excused himself from the ladies and beelined for his cronies, who were taking turns bellowing their respective catchphrases and generally making a scene. Or, it would've been a scene if they'd been anywhere else than a retired pro-wrester's birthday party.

"So, did you meet Lee yet? Max's girlfriend."

"No, but I know her. Well, not actually *know* her. I ran into her at the doctor's office a couple weeks ago."

Ten left out the rest.

"Well, how about that, huh? It's like you two were destined to meet."

"Why is that?"

"Turns out she's looking for a place to rent, and you happen to have a guest house available. Your dad already said yes, now it's just up to you."

The set ended and Max walked Lee over to Ten. Nick joined them, too.

Max said, "Hey guys. I think all of you have met Lee by now, except for—"

"Tenley!"

They all turned to see Josh striding toward them, his face a mask of determination and single-mindedness.

Ten said, "Josh, what are you doing here? Are you all right?"

Lee said, "Your name is Tenley? That's crazy, my name is—"

Another shout interrupted. "Lee! Tenley Harper! Where are you?"

Both women yelled, "I'm over here."

Nick said, "Hey, I know that guy. He claimed he was married to you."

"He's not married to her," said Lee, looking down. "He's married to me."

Max looked from the man to Lee and said, "I don't understand, Lee. What is happening here?"

"Yeah, and who let this clown in? This is a private party, pal," said Nick to Josh.

Josh, ignoring Nick, said, "Tenley Harper, I love you. I'm a way better choice than this bozo."

The tall man who kind of looked like Ryan Gosling said, "I thought you were seeing the guitar guy. You're seeing this guy, too?"

Lee stammered, "Wh-I—no, of course not. He's my trainer."

Max raised his hands to halt the back and forth volleying between everyone. "Wait a minute. You're both named Tenley Harper? That's impossible. You said your last name is Merriweather, not Harper."

Lee opened her mouth, but no sound came out.

Nick said, "Ten is with me now, buddy. Back off."

The tall man threw his hands in the air. "Jesus, Lee, you're seeing this guy, too?"

Ten said, "No, *I'm* seeing *him*," she wagged her thumb at Nick, "and *she's* seeing *him*," she pointed at Max.

Everyone talked at once. Ten looked at Lee. Lee looked at Ten. While everyone yelled and finger jabbed at each other, Ten ducked down, grabbed Lee's hand and pulled her toward the gate leading to the beach.

Once on the other side, they stopped and looked back, then locked gazes. Ten tipped her head toward the beach. Lee nodded. The two ran hand in hand—and resembling opposing chess pieces—down the shoreline until the lights from the party were out of sight.

They fell only the sand, heedless of their dresses and panting.

"Is your name really Tenley Harper?"

"Yup. Yours?"

"Yep. What's your middle name? Mine's Rose."

Lee smiled. "Found the difference. Mine's Grace. What are the odds?"

Ten shook her head. "Sounds like the beginning of a joke. Two women with the same name walk into the same doctor's office on the same day…"

"Then meet up again weeks later at a party thrown by one of those women. Not quite a punchline, I guess."

"Lee? Do you think there's a chance they might have mixed—"

"I think there's a very good chance they did, Ten."

Ten, her eyes on the crashing waves, reached out and took her new friend's hand. They would know everything soon enough. By silent agreement, the pair stayed put and watched the tide roll away.

<u>27</u> THE TWO TENLEYS

On their slow walk back to the house Lee and Ten discovered there was little else they had in common aside from their names and hair color. Lee learned Ten's life was the absolute opposite of her own. She also confessed her admiration for the 'hippie woman' from the doctor's office.

"You're kidding me," said Ten.

"Nope. I left that office feeling like I had a new lease on life. Like, I don't know, God said, 'Here's your chance, Lee. Don't blow it.' Next thing I knew, I was telling my husband I want a divorce and trying to emulate a woman I met for less than five minutes."

"Me? That's so—"

"Crazy?"

"Flattering. Honestly, Lee, I feel like a fraud. This whole free spirit thing? The reality is, I'm just as scared and uncertain as the next person. I mean, I don't even travel."

She spun around; her arms wide. "This is the extent of my universe. By choice. And you know what else? I've been avoiding relationships for so long, I don't even know *how* to be in one."

Lee gave her a sympathetic smile. "Yeah, but you are in one now, though. Looks like it's going pretty well, too."

Ten snorted. "That's because we both think I'm dying. What happens if I'm not? What then?"

"Well, then it means I'm dying, I guess."

Ten stopped walking. "Fuck."

Lee stopped, too. "Yeah. Fuck."

They reached the gate to the pool and let themselves in. The party had ended and only seven figures took up the chairs around the fire pit.

Nick was the first to speak. "The two Tenleys have returned. Welcome back, ladies."

He pulled out a chair for Ten and Max pulled one out for Lee. It relieved and gratified her to see him.

"You stayed," whispered Lee.

Max nodded; his expression grim. Lee's heart sank. He was likely staying just long enough to tell her goodbye.

Charlie, in his gruff baritone, asked, "You kids all right?"

Lee and Ten exchanged glances, then bobbed their heads. They were as okay as could be, given the Twilight Zone aspect their lives had taken on. Margot spoke next.

"This is just... surreal. This whole thing."

A pregnant pause followed. Ten at last spoke. "I'm sorry, but who are you?"

All heads turned to a rail thin brunette sitting back from the rest. Nervous looks passed between Ten's father, Nick, Margot, and the thin woman. Nick cleared his throat.

"I can explain, Harper."

Lee looked from the woman to Ten. Wasn't it obvious who the woman was? The resemblance— though she favored her father more—was clear.

As their drama unfolded, so did Lee's.

"Lee, we need to talk," said Kenny, his body turned to block Max's view.

Max edged in front of Kenny. "We also need to talk, Lee."

"I think what I have to say is more important," said Kenny.

"Oh, is that so?" said Max.

Her head pounding, Lee whispered, "Can you two stop it please?"

"Yeah, that is so. That's my *wife*, Mister."

"Well, for the past three weeks, she's been *my* girlfriend and there's been no mention of *you*, buddy."

"Well, that's probably because she has a brain tumor, so she's not acting right."

All the other chatter stopped. Dead silence but for the scrape of Lee's chair as she stood. Ten, Nick, and Max stood slowly, too. Kenny dropped his head in his hand.

"Did you say I—"

Black dots filled Lee's peripheral vision. Her last conscious image was of Max's stricken face staring down at her and his strong arms cradling her limp body.

[28] TEN

Ten and Nick sat in silence in the hospital waiting area. Max and Kenny wore tracks in the carpet from pacing opposite sides of the room. Back home, Charlie, Kablooey, and Margot were with the woman who Ten intuited to be her biological mother, even before Nick could confess his ill thought out plan.

"So, this turned out to be a crazy night, huh?"

"Sure did, Keller."

"You, uh, okay?"

"Well. I thought I had a terminal illness for the past three weeks, found out tonight I don't. So, that's cool. Oh, and my biological mother, who gave me up as an infant and never tried to see me in thirty-six years, is right now at my house. Not sure how to feel about that one, Keller."

Nick looked down at the floor. "Fair enough, Harper."

"H-how about this? One minute you're dating a dying woman, the next, poof, she's alive."

"Just like Frankenstein's monster." Nick chuckled. Ten didn't. "Kidding, Harper. What's wrong?"

"I dunno." She looked away.

"You're doing that thing you do when you're anxious."

Ten scowled. "Shut up. What thing?"

"The hair twirly thing."

She dropped her hand from her hair. "No, I'm not."

After another long silence, she said, "You're off the hook, Keller."

He twisted in his seat to face her. "Off the hook? What does that mean?"

Ten inhaled, then said it as quickly as she could. "You don't have to be with me anymore if you don't want to."

"Harper, you *sure* you don't have a brain tumor? What the hell are you trying to say? That I'm only with you because I thought you were dying? Like it was some kind of pity thing? Or, what, that I'm trying to be a martyr?"

"The thought has crossed my mind."

"Jesus. How are you this thick? I fucking love you, Harper. I want to marry you. I want us to have babies that look like you but maybe don't act as crazy as you do. I—"

"Was that a proposal, Keller? If so, you'll have to do better than that."

"No, that was not a propos—wait, are you saying you'd say yes?"

"Don't know. Haven't been asked."

Nick scraped his fingers through his hair. "I'm *not* asking. I was making a point."

"That you love me, and want to marry me, and have crazy little babies together."

"Not *crazy* babies. Beautiful babies."

They sat side by side. Nick grinned down at the ceiling, Ten down the corridor. She never had a sparring partner before. This—her and Nick Keller—had the potential to be great fun.

"Well, you can sit here and pout. I'll see if those two needs anything," said Ten.

"No, you sit. I'll check on them."

"I can—"

Both men spoke in unison. "We're fine."

Ten and Nick blinked at them.

Max said, "You two aren't as quiet as you think. Congrats, by the way. Bout time you kids got together."

They muttered their thanks and sat in chagrined silence. After what seemed like an eternity, the doctor came out. Kenny and Max stopped their pacing and stared at him. They spoke at the same time.

"How is she? Can I see her?"

The doctor looked at the foursome and said, "Are you all Mrs. Harper's family?"

They looked to Kenny, who looked at each of them, his gaze staying longest on Max, before saying, "Yes. I'm her husband. They're her family."

"Very well. Let's sit, shall we?"

Kenny and Max sat like two obedient school children, keeping several chairs distance.

"First, I'm Dr. Chen. As I understand it, Mrs. Harper's prior care was... mishandled due to a series of unfortunate events. Dr. Rue has apprised me of those unusual circumstances and requested I take over. Is that satisfactory?"

"Yes," said Kenny. "How long does she have, Dr. Chen?"

"One step at a time, son. Mrs. Harper has a type of tumor called glioblastoma. It's often aggressive, fast moving, and tremendously difficult to treat.

Frequent headaches are the first symptom, but usually go ignored or misdiagnosed. A host of other symptoms usually follow. Cognitive impairment, memory loss—"

Kenny jumped in. "Erratic behavior, too. Right?"

"Ah, yes, all depending on the glioblastoma's location in the brain."

Kenny gave Max a smug nod. Here, the doctor paused and appeared to be weighing his words. He steepled his fingers under his chin.

"Your wife's first imaging—five weeks ago—showed a sizable tumor in her temporal lobe. At her follow up appointment, she should have been presented with the unfortunate facts of her condition."

Ten interrupted. "That she only had six to ten months to live."

Dr. Chen looked at her. "That's correct. You're the... *other* Tenley Harper, aren't you?"

Tenley raised her hand. "Present."

Dr. Chen gave a terse smile. "Yes, well, what should have happened next was the scheduling of another round of imaging, follow up appointments, and a plan for hospice care. Did you do any of that, Miss Harper?"

Ten grimaced. "No, not exactly. I, uh, ignored the calls from the doctor's office. I guess I just didn't see the point."

"Didn't see the—okay, well, what's done is done. I do suggest, Mis Harper, you schedule an appointment and make sure your health is what it appears to be."

Max broke in. "Uh, no offense—Ten, Doc—but can we get back to Lee now?"

"Right." said Dr. Chen. "As I was saying, follow up imaging would have been beneficial to note the tumor's progression, but Mrs. Harper *also* ignored the calls from the doctor's office. So, we have no subsequent imaging aside from the original and those taken here this morning."

Another pause, this time Ten could swear he looked perplexed. They all leaned forward.

"There's no other way to say this, but it appears Mrs. Harper's tumor has shrunk by a significant degree."

They spoke all at once.

"It shrunk?"

"You mean she's getting better?"

"Holy shit."

"She's going to live, right?"

"Slow down, slow down, everyone. This is superb news, yes. Highly uncommon, too. We still need to keep her for observation and more testing. But, yes. If the tumor is shrinking, there is a strong likelihood of Mrs. Harper's survival."

Ten hugged both Kenny and Max. Nick shook their hands and clapped them on the back. They all thanked the doctor, who looked from Kenny to Max several times before excusing himself.

"One person can visit, but only for a short time. We want her to rest up. I'll, uh, let you folks decide who'll be going in."

Awkward stillness ensued. Nick and Ten looked everywhere but at Max and Kenny.

"Well, you are her husband, so..." Max trailed off.

"Right, yeah. Thanks for understanding. Well, I, uh..."

It was painful to watch, and Ten's heart broke for Max. She even felt sorry for Lee's husband, even though she barely knew him.

When Kenny walked away, Nick said to Max, "If it's any consolation, man, he's a good dude. She'll be in good hands."

"Yeah, I suppose so," said Max.

"Wait, what?" Ten looked from one to the other, incredulous. "That's it? You're just giving up and walking away? You're in love with her. She's in love with you. You can't just *walk away*."

Max ruffled her hair and smiled sadly. "Au contraire, mon petite Cherie. I think it's the only thing I can do. Fifteen years of marriage versus three weeks of... sheer joy—at least on my end—doesn't compare."

"But—" Ten wasn't ready to give it up.

"It was the tumor, Ten. That's why she left her husband and quit her job, and hooked up with me, and..."

Ten hugged her dear, sad friend. It was all she could think of doing.

Nick patted his back. "Sorry, bro. Really am."

With a sniff and a half-hearted laugh, Max said, "Come on, now. Let's go to Cappy's and get shnockered."

"I think I'll meet you two there. I've got a situation to handle back home, thanks to this guy,"

She elbowed Nick's side none too gently. He oofed, and said, "Yeah, sorry about that, babe."

Max said, "Ah, that's right. Your... mom. Go easy, kid. Never know what it's like in someone else's shoes."

Ten sent them off but instead of leaving, she lingered in the lobby. When Kenny came out of Lee's room, she slipped in. She *had* to speak to her.

Ten deflated when she saw Lee's eyes were closed. It would be wrong to wake her after her ordeal. It would have to wait. She turned to leave.

"Is he gone?"

Ten spun around. "You're awake?"

Lee smiled. "Yeah, I'm not ready to talk to Kenny yet. So, you know..."

"You fake slept. I get it. So, you, uh, doing okay?"

Lee sat up, clear-eyed and animated. "Considering? Yeah, I feel good. It's all so crazy, though, isn't it? First, I thought I had a brain tumor, find out I *don't* have one, then find out I *do* have one, *and* it's terminal. *Now* I'm being told the tumor is shrinking."

Ten went to speak but Lee carried on.

"I quit my job, left my husband, got a tattoo, met a great guy, started singing, made new friends, and oh, met a woman with the same exact name. What am I forgetting?'

Ten chuckled. "I think that about covers it all except… now what? Are you going back to your husband? Or—"

"I kind of have to, I think."

Ten didn't agree. "Why? You left him for a reason, Lee. Nothing against him, but you and Max seem so perfect together. I know he loves you."

"And I love *him*, Ten. At least I think I do. But what if its all been because of the tumor? What if, even though it's shrinking, it's pressing on some—I don't know—nerve or something, and it's making me do crazy things?"

She looked around the room and put her hands in the air. "I mean, look at everything I just did. It reeks of crazy."

"So, you're just going back to your old life."

"It's the right thing to do."

"It's the safe thing to do," corrected Ten.

Was she being fair? She'd never been married... or even in a relationship longer than six months. Who was she to tell this woman what to do? Before Ten could say more, Lee spoke.

Lee averted her gaze. "Tell Max I... tell him I'm sorry. For everything, For the pain I've caused, for..."

"I'll tell him, Lee. You have my number and know where to find us. I guess this is goodbye, Tenley Grace Harper. And good luck."

"Same to you, Tenley Rose Harper."

29 THREE MONTHS LATER: TEN

"It feels strange to be back home, doesn't it? Were those trees always there?"

"Harper, we were gone two weeks."

"Shut up, Keller. And it's Harper-Keller to you, thank you very much."

"Is your dad gonna kick my ass for eloping with you?"

Ten shrugged. "Probably. He always wanted to throw a big, lavish wedding for me."

"God damn it, Harper. You said in Greece he'd be fine with it."

"I lied. Or, *maybe* I'm lying now. Hmm. What will the Hurricane do? The suspense is killing me."

Ten flutterer her fingertips together and laughed her most maniacal laugh. Nick pursed his lips and tightened his grip on the steering wheel.

"Does Tomi Lyn know?"

"I *may* have called her from the airport."

Ten and Tomi Lyn were trying on a relationship for size. Ten wasn't ready to call her 'mom' and maybe never would. But she couldn't deny the way it made her feel, getting to know her mother. It was like she'd spent thirty-six years trying to find a missing puzzle piece and then, poof, there it was. They shared the same wicked sense of humor, a passion for the arts, a proclivity toward anything outdoors, and a love of animals.

The last commonality broke the ice that first meeting. Ten had returned home to find Tomi Lyn by the pool, Fitz by her side and Lizzy on her lap. She held, of all things, Pride and Prejudice in her hands.

"You're a Jane Austen fan?"

Tomi Lyn had set the book down and studied Ten's face. "Yep. You look so much like your dad. A pretty version of him, that is."

Ten laughed through her nose. "So, I've been told my whole life."

"You must think I'm the worst person in the world. What kind of woman gives up their kid and disappears, right?"

In a neutral tone, Ten said, "You had your reasons, it sounds like. To be honest? I don't know how I feel about you. I think, maybe, I should hate you. Or at least resent you. But I've had a great life, Tomi Lyn. Charlie is the best dad, the best parent, any kid could ever have."

Tomi Lyn flinched a little. Whether at the use of her given name, or crediting her father for everything, Ten didn't know. She didn't feel sorry, either. She only stated the facts. Still, she softened the blow.

"I believe you loved me enough to give me the best life possible. I have to believe that, because it would otherwise mean you didn't give a shit about me."

Tomi Lyn reached out to place a hand on Ten's arm, then thought better. She stroked Lizzy's back instead.

"No, Tenley. It wasn't that I didn't care. You had it right the first guess. I loved you from the second I saw you. I tried real hard to straighten out the mess I'd gotten into. But it just got worse and worse."

Tomi Lyn's voice shook, and she looked far off towards the beach. When she continued, she sounded a million miles away.

"We were living in the basement of an abandoned building. I had that post-partum going on, but I didn't know it. I just knew that my life had spiraled out of control and I couldn't even take care of myself, let alone a baby."

"So, you brought me to Charlie."

Tomi Lyn nodded. "I always knew you were his. Bobby couldn't have kids, something I *didn't* know until I told him I was pregnant." She gave an ironic laugh. "I bet on the wrong horse. Your dad was the better man in every way, and I picked the jerk."

"It must've been hard for you, leaving your baby... me."

"You don't know the half of it. Nor does it matter. Let's just say things got a hell of a lot worse before they got better."

"What changed? When?"

"About five years went by. I ended up in Connecticut of all places. Followed some loser who said he had family here that would take us in. He dumped me as soon as we crossed the state line. I hitchhiked across a dozen towns—no destination in mind, really—till this nice couple pick me up. They had four dogs and a pygmy goat in the truck—" She stopped and laughed at the memory, "and said if I didn't mind riding with all the animals, they'd bring me home with them. They took in all kinds of strays, even human ones."

Ten smiled, but it horrified her to imagine anyone living such a bleak life.

"Anyhow, they had a little farm in Rocky Hill. Let me stay in their renovated barn in exchange for helping with the animals. I got cleaned up and straightened out, thanks to those animals."

She said that the husband received a job offer in Pennsylvania too good to refuse. Around the same time, an anonymous donor funded the rescue. So, they offered a small salary to Tomi Lyn if she'd run the non-profit and stay in the house. Ten years ago, after saving up everything she could, she made them an offer and they accepted it.

"By the grace of God, those people came into my life. But I suppose you're wondering why I never reached out to you or your dad, aren't you?"

"Yes. Why didn't you?"

Tomi Lyn shook her head. "In the beginning, I believed I'd get you back. I was gonna clean up, get my girl, get on with it. But time kept moving. It was moving so fast, Tenley. One minute, only a day had gone by. Next, it was a year. A *year*, and I hadn't seen or held my child. Then it was two. And—well, you get the idea."

Tomi Lyn scrubbed her face roughly with her hands and heaved a ragged breath.

"I psyched myself out. That's what it was. I started thinking about all I'd missed. Your first tooth. Your first steps. First word. Then I thought, *'She won't even know who I am. She's gonna cry when I hold her. He's her mom and her dad now. Not me.'* Every time I picked up the phone to call or looked at airfare to fly down to see you, those thoughts snuck into my head. Until, at some point, I just figured you were much better off without me in your life."

Too many emotions flooded Ten's mind. Hurt. Disappointment. Sadness. Understanding. Sympathy. Anger. All of it. All that lost time, for fear of the unknown. What a waste of precious time.

But was she all that different from Tomi Lyn? Wasn't fear of the unknown holding *her* back? She remembered her conversation with Lee on the beach. Everyone saw her as a free spirit—a hippie woman, as Lee called her—but she was a coward. Hiding behind a mask of indifference to avoid getting attached to anyone. Never straying far from home, from her safety net. She'd let time slip away, too, and not even the belief she was dying had changed it. Right then, she decided *no more*. It was time to live.

Tenley Harper planned on taking life by the horns. Grudges, hard feelings, negativity, and fear had no place. She felt as free as everyone perceived her to be. In the spirit of enlightenment, Tenley vowed to give Tomi Lyn a chance.

"Well, you're in my life now. I'd like to get to know you, Tomi Lyn. If it's what you want, too."

"I do. But I-I'm afraid you'll be disappointed."

"Tell you what. Let's not put any expectations on each other, okay? We'll just give it a try and see where it goes. Deal?"

"Deal. Your boyfriend must have good intuition. My return flight isn't until next week."

"Oh, don't give him too much credit. He got lucky, is all. I'll think of a good payback for blindsiding me. No offense."

"None taken. And I had a feeling that was the case, so I took the liberty of bringing some payback with me."

Tomi Lyn's mischievous grin made Tenley laugh. "Wow, we really are related, huh? What'd you do?"

"Well, he called me under some ruse he was looking to adopt a dog. So, I brought him one."

"You brought him a dog? No way."

"Yes way. He's a three-year-old St. Bernard named Ludo, and he weighs in at a petite one-hundred and sixty-five pounds."

Ten covered her mouth, laughing. "Oh, I can't wait to see the look on his face when he sees him."

"I can't wait to see his face when he has to pick up after him," said Tomi Lyn.

A tentative bond, one that began over a shared enjoyment of tormenting Nick, formed that first night. Over the following weeks they exchanged phone calls and video chatted, and Tenley even booked a flight to visit her mother in the fall. She heard autumn in New England was a sight to behold.

Nick surprised them both by falling instantly in love with Ludo, and the feeling was mutual. Tomi Lyn cancelled Ludo's return flight—one she'd booked just in case—and gave him training tips. Turned out he was a natural, despite never having a dog in his whole life.

Nick's voice brought her out of her reverie. "You think Ludo will remember me?"

"I'm sure he will. Besides, you made Lucy video chat almost every day."

"You're just jealous you didn't think of it first."

"Okay Keller. Whatever you say." Ten rolled her eyes for good measure.

Soon the familiar shoreline burst into view and a surge of joy flooded Ten's heart. Traveling had fulfilled an unrealized need in her, and she'd relished the foreign sights, sounds, tastes and smells. But there nothing compared to the comfort and belonging of *home*.

"Nick? Is it weird that I'm so content to stay in one place?"

"Nah. Makes perfect sense. You traveled all over the place as a kid, right? So, you go one extreme or the other. Either you live like a nomad because it's all you know, or you settle down and stay put."

He sent a side glance and a smirk in her direction.

"Leave it to you, Harper to look like a nomad but live like a hermit."

Ten looked down at her outfit. Cowboy hat, tube top, peasant skirt, tennis sneaker. She shrugged. "I prefer gypsy, thank you very much."

"Whatever you say, wife."

"Holy shit, Keller. I'm a wife. You're a husband. Who'd have thought the hippie and the bachelor would end up together? This is so weird."

"But awesome, though, right?"

"I'll give you that. It is. And so are you."

Nick smiled and took his wife's hand. He slowed over the bridge so she could take in her beloved coastline. Ten powered down all the windows and tossed her hat in the back, letting the wind sing through her hair. She felt... *alive*.

³⁰ THREE MONTH LATER: LEE

From her bed, Lee watched the ceiling fan's slow spin. Kenny had flicked the switch on his way out. An act of habit. He'd come in to check on her before leaving for work, and Lee feigned sleep.

She heard him breathing from the doorway, smelled his cologne—new, one she'd never smelled on him before—and sensed his hesitation. It had been like this since they came home from the hospital. Neither knew how to act or what to say. So, they danced around each other, dodged one another, and made nothing more than halting small talk.

Dr. Chen ordered her to rest and to have as little stress put upon her until... well, no one was sure what *until* meant. Until her normalness came back? Until the tumor returned? She waited with pragmatic patience. She would behave like her old self again. Her mind would not drift over and over back to Max, her heart would not stutter at the image of his face behind her closed eyes. Kenny's new look and attitude would grow on her. He would grow on her, like he had all those years ago.

Lee waited until the front door closed before getting up. At the bedroom window, she watched his car back out, then head toward the school. At least one of them kept their job. She made it halfway down the stairs when a wave of nausea forced her to sit.

She'd been experiencing these fluttery ripples and the accompanying watery mouth and constricting throat feelings for a few weeks. Something to do with the tumor, she supposed. When she met with Dr. Chen in the afternoon, she mention it.

This would be her third scan in as many months. So far, the tumor continued to shrink. She blamed her symptoms—the nausea and exhaustion—on rapid changes happening inside her brain. Tenley had laughed with a bitter irony when Dr. Chen asked if she'd like to do a pregnancy test.

"I'm infertile, Dr. Chen, so thank you, but no."

He'd opened his mouth, perhaps to ask again, but Lee turned and walked out the door. *Pregnant.* How absurd. Fourteen years of trying, of hoping and wishing, and of disappointment. She didn't mention it to Kenny. They barely talked at all, aside from polite civilities. Two people who'd shared a life but now were strangers.

When two o'clock came, she'd already been in the doctor's waiting room for twenty minutes, her purse on her lap, knees pressed together, eyes cast down. Her phone chimed, a text message from Tenley. Lee grinned as she read it.

Put your purse on the floor. Sit back. Relax.
Call me after if you want to talk.
xo Tenley Too

They'd not only stayed in touch since that bizarre, surreal night, but a genuine friendship and bond formed between them. Before Lee could type a response, Tenley rapid-fired another message.

Guest house is still vacant.

And then another.

Our mutual friend is doing okay.
 We're all keeping him busy.

Lee waited a beat before answering.

Thank you. Perfect timing. Nervous,
But okay, I guess. Tell him

She deleted the last two words.

Give everyone my love. Call you in an
Hour.
Xo Tenley, Too

Max's beautiful, sweet face appeared before her closed eyes and she willed it away. Her feelings for him weren't real, it was the brain tumor making her act unlike herself. It had to be that. Otherwise, it would mean she walked away from what could be the love of her life.

"Mrs. Harper? Dr. Chen is ready to see you."

Despite the almost routine nature of these visits, Lee feared bad news each time. This visit was no different. Wobbly legs carried her to the office at the end of a long, blue and white striped corridor of numbered exam rooms.

"Lee, good to see you. Have a seat."

Dr. Chen stood and gestured to one of the two leather chairs opposite his desk and came around to join her. He had a file folder under his arm. Once the door closed behind the nurse, Dr. Chen spoke.

"Okay, I won't keep you in suspense. Your last scan continues to show tumor shrinkage. Another centimeter, to be precise. Lee, it's amazing. Your first scan showed a tumor roughly the size of a lime. It's now the size of a pea."

Lee exhaled. "Thank you, Dr. Chen. I'm so relieved."

"Now, how are you feeling? Still experiencing the nausea? How's your energy?"

"Same. No better, no worse."

He stared at her a moment, assessing her. "Lee, I think you should reconsider taking that pregnancy test. We can do it here, lab is on-site."

"I told you, I—"

"Humor me, Lee. Please?"

"Fine. Tell the nurse to give me a cup, I guess."

"Actually, I'd like to do a blood test. Okay with you?"

"Why not? I've been a pin cushion for fourteen years, what's one more poke?"

Dr. Chen called in the nurse, who took her to an exam room. Lee chatted rapid bursts.

"I don't know why I'm agreeing to this."

The nurse smiled. "Arm, please."

"I mean, it's absurd. My husband and I haven't—"

"Just a little pinch."

"I had coffee this morning. I don't know if that matters, but—"

"It doesn't. You're all set, Mrs. Harper. Would you like to return to Dr. Chen's office? You're the last patient of the day."

Lee nodded and followed the young nurse back down the hall. She knew the results and denied herself the candle flicker of hope. While she waited, she checked her phone. A message, from Kenny.

How was the appointment?

She responded.

Fine. All good

She shoved the phone back in her purse. Not for the first time, she mused about her feelings for him. His transformation, impressive. His new sense of confidence and assertiveness, even more impressive. It should please her. It was what she wanted from him all along, and yet... she felt nothing. Not even when the waitress at the restaurant last week blatantly flirted with him. Or when the woman in the grocery store kept making eyes at him.

Lee couldn't even feign jealousy or concern, nor could Kenny seem to care if she did. They were treading water and they both knew it. So why were they afraid to pull the plug? What push did they need?

"Lee, thanks for waiting."

Dr. Chen breezed into the room, his cologne—normal a scent she found pleasant—made her throat constrict. She plastered a benign smile a blank expression in her face as he sat down. For a moment he just stared at her, his dark brows drawn close together.

"It's okay, Dr. Chen. I'm used to hearing the words. You don't—"

"Lee, you're pregnant. I'd say about three months along."

Lee remained statue-still, her hands on the arms of her chair. At last she said, "I'm sorry, what did you say?"

"You're pregnant. Three months, give or take. We can pinpoint better, though. Lee, have you been having any other indications of pregnancy? Breast tenderness? Mild cramping? Changes in appetite?"

Lee looked away and nodded. Yes, to all. She either ignored or justified each to herself, never allowing for the possibility of—

"I'm... pregnant. But how is it—"

"It's not as uncommon as you might think. Sometimes, when the pressure to conceive is eased, and your mind and body have time to relax, magic happens. Not a very scientific statement, I realize. I do think science comes into play in relation to your tumor and your pregnancy. The effects of hormones on your brain can be profound."

Dr. Chen droned on about estrogen and progesterone and brain cells, but Lee had stopped listening. She was pregnant with Max's child. There was no question in her mind whose baby it was. Lee's instinct told her to get up and run to Max as fast as she could. Her logic kept her rooted to the spot.

"I-I've had several miscarriages, Dr. Chen. What are the chances of... you know?"

Dr. Chen's face filled with understanding and sympathy, further confirming for Lee that he was not only a great doctor, but a good man.

"Then you well know there are no guarantees. This will sound trite, I know, but relax. Take your prenatal vitamins, carry on with life as usual, and schedule an appointment with your OBGYN as soon as possible. I'd like to stay in close contact with both your obstetrician and you as your pregnancy progresses."

"If my p-pregnancy progresses," corrected Lee.

He smiled and came around the desk. "*As your pregnancy develops*, Lee. Think positive."

He extended his hand to help her up and on impulse, she hugged him.

"Thank you, Dr. Chen. For everything."

He chuckled. "Easy now, this isn't goodbye. It's see you in a month for your next scan."

She waited until in the car before pulling out her phone, her hands shaking as she typed the text.

You around? Could use a friendly ear.

Within a minute, Tenley's response.

Of course. Git your ass over here.

I'm home. Poolside, come around back

Lee stretched the seatbelt over her waist and paused, looking down at her stomach. There was a baby in there. A baby. Hers and Max's child. *Max.* Her heart clenched. *Oh, Max.*

31 TENLEY TOO

Ten sat where she said she'd be, poolside on a lounge chair. She wore a black string bikini that revealed almost ever ridiculously perfect inch of her tan body, and the widest brim black hat Lee had ever seen. But instead of laying back and reading or resting, Ten straddled the lounger, a laptop open between her knees.

Lee watched for a moment as her friend tapped at the keys in rapid bursts, gazed off into the distance, then tapped another flurry of words. How would she say it? Should she even tell Ten? Maybe waiting until she got further along would be better. She opened the gate and called out a hello.

"Hey chica. That was fast," said Ten as Lee sat beside her. "Mimosa? Or, would you prefer a Bloody Mary?"

"I'm pregnant," blurted Lee.

A slow grin spread across Ten's face. The smile infected Lee, and suddenly she grinned, too. It was the first time she allowed herself to fell any sense of joy or excitement.

"So, no mimosa, huh?"

Lee laughed, "How about a virgin mimosa?"

Ten slapped her laptop shut and sprang up. "Come on, mama. Let's go inside and get you a glass of champagne-less orange juice."

"Hello, Mr. Hurri—Mr. Harp—"

"Call me Charlie, sweetheart. Hell, you got the same name as my girl, ya might as well call me Dad, too."

Lee's eyed welled. Charlie, alarmed, looked at Ten and mouthed, "What'd I do wrong?"

Ten narrowed her eyes at her father, jerked her head at Lee and mouthed, "Give her a hug."

Charlie jumped into action, gave Lee a fatherly hug and pat on the head. "How about I make my famous pancakes?"

Lee sniffled and said, "That would be amazing. Just so, so amazing."

Ten masked her laugh with a cough. "Okay, honey. You sit, I'll pour, and Dad will cook."

Once they were all at the table, Charlie said, "All right girls. Spill it. What's going on with Tenley Too over here?"

"My tumor is still shrinking, and I still want to divorce my husband. I miss being here by the ocean. Oh, and I'm pregnant with Max's baby."

"You maybe should've led with that one, kid," said Charlie.

Ten bit her bottom lip, then said, "Don't be offended, but are you sure it's—"

"It's Max's. I'm one hundred percent positive," said Lee.

Ten clapped. "That's great news, Lee. Have you told him yet?"

"No. I-I wouldn't even know what to say to him. It's been months since we've spoken, and the way they left things... oh, I can't bear to think about it. He must hate me."

"He doesn't hate you, honey."

"How do you know? Did he say that?"

"Not in so many words. But I can tell," said Tenley.

Lee looked to Charlie. "What do you think? Wouldn't you hate the woman who lied to you and broke your heart?"

Charlie scratched his head. "Well, I'd say, knowing Max like we all do, I doubt the man has the capacity to hate anyone. I'm guessing he's feeling pretty low, though."

"And you have just the news to cheer him up," added Ten.

Charlie put a hand up to slow his daughter's enthusiasm "Hang on, now. If you don't mind my saying, I think you need to tie up some loose ends first."

Lee nodded and looked down. "You mean Kenny. You're right." She searched Ten's eyes. "You won't tell Max until I'm ready?"

"It'll kill me, but, yes. I'll keep quiet. But hurry, will ya?"

Ten jumped up and hugged Lee to show she was teasing, and Lee relaxed. She dreaded the talk with Kenny, but it had to be done.

The two Tenleys spent the rest of the afternoon poolside, where they exchanged stories, compared upbringings, and considered their futures.

"Do you and Nick want children?"

Ten shrugged one shoulder and frowned. "I don't know. I mean, we've talked about it. But, honestly? I don't know if I'm mom material. I-I never had one growing up, so I wouldn't have the slightest idea how to *be* one."

"Are you kidding me," asked Lee. "You'd be an amazing mother. I mean it. You'd be the cool mom that every other kid wished their mom could be more like."

"Yeah, maybe." Ten laughed. "*You're* going to be an awesome mom, Lee. Maybe if I watch you for a while, I'll pick up some pointers."

"Well, don't wait too long. I want our little ones to grow up together."

Ten's face broke into a wide smile. "That'd be kind of fantastic, wouldn't it?"

When the sun began its slow set, Lee stood to leave. The friends hugged and said their goodbyes. Ten extracted a promise to call or at least text after she'd spoken to Kenny.

On the long ride home, she rehearsed what she'd say and wondered how he'd take the news for the second time that she wanted a divorce. She knew how it made her feel. Sad. Sorry. And relieved.

32 KENNY

Kenny pulled a dinner plate from the microwave and set it on the kitchen table. As he placed his glass of water by the plate, he glanced at the clock on the wall. Seven-thirteen. Lee's appointment had been at two-thirty, yet she still wasn't home nearly five hours later. No call, no text. No, '*Hey, I'm okay, just out doing stuff.*' Was she with *him*?

He cut the grilled and reheated chicken breast, speared a potato, then chewed. He should feel angry, yet he didn't. Hurt and betrayal lacked, too. Kenny felt... nothing. He sipped his water, glanced again at the clock. Seven-twenty-three. The garage door whined open. A few minutes later, Lee walked in.

"Hey," said Lee.

"Hey," said Kenny.

"You found the chicken."

"Yep. Thanks for making a plate for me."

"No problem."

Silence. Lee hung her keys on the peg by the door and dropped her purse on the counter. Kenny continued to eat his dinner, although now he could taste nothing.

"Hungry?"

"No, I ate with Ten. I, uh, went to visit her."

"That's nice."

Lee inched closer to the kitchen table and rested her hand on the back of a chair.

"Yeah, it was. She and Nick eloped. They'll have a big reception, though."

"That's great. Good for them," said Kenny. "You, uh, want to sit down?"

"I—yes. I was hoping we could talk, Kenny."

Kenny's fork paused mid-air. He took the bite, put down the fork, and pushed the plate away. After a long sip of water, he looked her in the eye.

"It's over, Lee. We've done our best, I think. But you and I both know. We're getting a divorce."

Lee reached across the table and rested her hand over his. He turned it over to clasp hers. They blinked back tears and offered sad smiles to one another.

"I'm so sorry, Kenny."

"You don't have to be sorry, Lee. You deserve to be happy and if that guy makes you feel that way, then…"

"You deserve to be happy, too. I don't know who helped you with all this—" She waved her free hand at him, "but you seem so much more confident now. And you look like an actor. I can't think of his name, but the ladies love him."

Kenny laughed. "So I've been told. You don't have to worry about me, Lee. I'll be fine."

"Hey, I think I'm hungry after all. You mind if I eat with you."

Kenny gave her a smile. "Sure, why not?"

She grabbed a salad from the fridge and sat back down. Like shy strangers, they conversed—at first, haltingly, then with more ease and comfort—about things they'd never discussed. For the first time in all their relationship, Kenny and Lee became friends.

<u>33</u> MAX

Max sat out on his front porch, strumming his guitar and looking out over the ocean. Jude snored by his feet, his hind leg twitching every so often. A Corona served as a paperweight for the notebook on the side table. The plan had been to work on new music, but Don't Let Me Down was all his fingers would play. Lee's face was all his brain could think about.

It'd be so easy if he could be angry with her. Hate her. Replace the void, the emptiness with coldness. But time had only sweetened her in his heart. Even if she never really loved him, he had loved *her*. Almost from the moment he saw her in the bar, with her delicate face and—

"Jesus, stop it," said Max aloud. Jude's head popped up. "Sorry, buddy. Come on, let's go inside."

He shooed Jude in first and had one foot over the threshold when a familiar voice stopped him.

"Hello, Max."

Jude tried to charge back through to great his old friend, but Max closed the door.

"Sorry, buddy. Stay inside." He turned around, steeling himself. "Hello, Lee."

His voice came out husky, as if he'd not spoken in days. He swallowed and stared at her. She was a beautiful as ever, perhaps even more so, but something seemed different about her. Her hair? It was longer. She twirled a strand and looked down. No, it was something else he couldn't put his finger on.

For a moment, he thought she would turn and leave, and he had to force himself to not run down the steps and hold her in his arms. *Play it cool, old man.* She came to set things right, apologize, and get closure. That's all.

"Do you... uh, want to sit?"

She nodded and came up the steps. Max gestured to a chair and sat across from her. Then he waited.

"You look good, Max. How have—how are you?"

"Me, I—you know, Keeping busy." He shrugged and picked at the hem of his shorts. "I heard you're doing well. Getting better, I mean. From Tenley. She mentioned..." he trailed off.

"Yeah, no, that's true. I-it's still shrinking. The tumor. My doctor said he's never personally witnessed anything like it. So..."

"Wow, that's—that's amazing. Really. I'm so relieved. For you, I mean. I'm sure you and your— I'm sure it's great news all around."

"Max?"

He looked away. Here's where the, *'I'm sorry about everything and I hope you'll have a nice life'* comes in.

"Kenny and I finalized our divorce last week. Amicably, not that it matters. Turns out the marriage was as over as when I first left him. The brain tumor didn't make me do it, it was because I knew there was something more out there. Some*one* more."

Max felt hot and cold at the same time. His ears tingled. For a moment, he thought he might be having a stroke. Yet, somehow, his words came out normal.

"You got a divorce?"

"Yes, Max. Tenley offered me the guest house, so I've been staying there the past month. I-I thought you should know."

"Ah, I see."

She was giving him the polite heads-up. His heart sang and broke at the notion of seeing her often. He must've stayed quiet too long, because Lee stood, looking pained.

"I should let you get back to..."

"Would you like something to drink?"

Now they were speaking at the same time.

Lee gave a tremulous smile and said, "A glass of water would be nice, if it's no trouble."

When he came back, something had changed in Lee's posture. She looked resolved and determined. He was right.

"Max, sit down, please. I have something I need to say to you."

"Lee, it's all right. You don't have to apologize. I-I'm not mad at you. I don't think I could ever be mad at you. I just wish you'd—well, that doesn't matter anymore, I suppose."

"Yes—no—I mean," she pursed her lips and squeezed her eyes shut a moment, then tried again, "Yes, I *am* sorry. So incredibly sorry for how I handled everything. There's no excuse, aside from a brain tumor. Sorry, bad humor."

She set her glass down and sat forward on the edge of her seat.

"What I'm trying to say, Max, is that I love you. I think maybe I have since the moment we met. I know I blew it, I lost your trust. But I couldn't forgive myself if I didn't at least tell you how I feel. How I *still* feel about you. There's also one other thing—"

"Did you just say you love me?"

If there was anything he learned from his wife's death, Max understood how precious a gift time was. To waste it on anger or dwell on hurt would be an affront to that gift. Max had lost too much already. He wouldn't lose this woman for a second time. He had to speak the words burning on his tongue. She started to talk.

"I—yes. Very much so," said Lee, her chin quivering. "And I'm only telling you this because you have a right to know, and not because I expect anything from you, but—"

He couldn't wait.

He said, "Marry me."

At the same moment, she said, "I'm pregnant... with your baby."

"What?"

"What did you say?"

Lee tilted her head to the right. Max tipped his to the left. They blinked at one another. They stood. Max tentatively placed one hand on her hip, the other over her belly. She covered his hands with hers.

"A baby? Our baby? But I thought you—"

"So did I. It turns out I have this little miracle baby to thank for my remission, too. I guess that means I have *you* to thank, too."

Max stepped closer, pressing his forehead to hers. The breeze swept her hair against his cheek and he inhaled deeply. He pulled back and cupped her face in his hands.

"I take back my proposal. Temporarily, that is. I want to do it right. Okay?"

Lee giggled. "Okay. But maybe we should try living together again first? We could always get married later, after the baby."

"I don't know if I can wait that long, sweetheart."

"Max, I'm due in four months. It's really not all that long."

"Four months? You're five months pregnant? Holy shit. Ah, fuck. Sorry little one," said Max to her stomach, "Daddy's got a potty mouth."

He began pacing, his fingers drumming his lips as he muttered.

"Four months. We need a crib. A room. We need a room for the baby. We'll clear out the office. Prenatal vitamins. One of those stroller things. Car seat! Child-proofing. Lee, we need to—"

Lee was laughing behind her hand. "Oh, Max. If you could see yourself right now."

He stopped at looked at her. Really *looked* at her. How could he have not seen what was different about her earlier? There was a softness, a fullness to her face where it once had been angular. Though her sundress fit loose, hiding the volleyball sized bump his hand had pressed against moments before, he could now see the larger swell of her breasts against the fabric.

A wave of love... and lust overcame him. With tender adoration, he said, "Sweetheart if *you* could only see yourself right now."

When they kissed, it was like a homecoming.

<u>PILOGUE ONE YEAR LATER</u>

The little bell above the salon door jangled as Lee walked in. A stunning, café-au-lait skinned, black-haired woman smiled and gave her a wave.

Lee asked, "Any chance you could take a walk-in?"

"Have a seat, I'll be with you in just a few minutes."

Lee waved and nodded, then grabbed a hairstyle magazine from the coffee table. Her hair—now well past her shoulders—hadn't been cut or styled in over a year. Between the pregnancy and taking care of little Rider, now four months old, she hadn't the time or care. But, like Tenley said, she was getting married in less than a week. She needed to look more like a bride and less like a banshee.

"Thanks for waiting. I'm Jacqui. Come on back and we'll talk about what you'd like to do today. Tea? Coffee?"

Lee sat in the chair. "Tea would be nice. Thanks for taking me without an appointment."

Jacqui brought her a steaming mug and began inspecting her hair.

"I'm Lee."

Jacqui, whose hands were lifting and separating Lee's hair, stilled. She met Lee's eyes in the mirror.

"I thought you looked kind of familiar," said Jacqui.

"Kenny has talked about you," said Lee.

Jacqui put her hands up and stepped back. "Listen, all I knew was you two were separated. And, for the record, nothing happened—"

"Jacqui, Kenny and I are divorced. Have been for about a year. I'm getting remarried this week."

"No shit? To the singer?"

Lee laughed. "Yes, to the singer. So, it's all fine. I mean it. Kenny and I are friends, believe it or not. And he *has* talked about you. Several times, as a matter of fact. Calls you the one that got away."

The corners of Jacqui's mouth twitched, but she tried to sound indifferent. "He said that, huh?"

"Yes. Now I can see why."

"Oh, stop. You're gorgeous. No wonder he tried to hang on to you."

"Actually, the divorce was very amicable. We both knew it was over. I think, for Kenny, meeting you was what helped him see it."

Jacqui chose to not respond, and instead said, "I think if we just take off these split ends, shape it up and add in a few soft highlights, you'll feel like a brand new you. Sound good?"

"Perfect."

They made small talk—the weather, business, the wedding plans.

"Beach wedding, huh? Those are always fun. I mean, I'm not a big fan of the sand, but the pictures are always beautiful."

It was on the tip of her tongue to say that Kenny hated the sand, too. But she held it. She wracked her brain for a way to bring him up without it being obvious. Jacqui beat her too it, though.

"So, did you invite your ex to the wedding? I'm sorry. None of my business. I don't know why I'd even say—"

"Yes, actually. He'll be there."

"Oh. That's nice."

She applied the color to Lee's hair, avoiding eye contact.

"You know," said Lee, "I don't think I'd be any good at styling my hair for the wedding. It has to be special, you know? Would you, by any chance, be available?"

A quick glace in the mirror. "I-I'd have to check my calendar. Hang on."

She went over to the reception desk and flipped through an appointment book, then came back and resumed her task.

"I'm available," was all she said.

Lee covered her grin by taking a sip of her tea. "Perfect."

When Lee left—feeling lighter and pretty—she gave Jacqui all the detail for the wedding and the time she'd need to arrive. The women parted, one feeling self-satisfied and the other uncertain.

***

Nick sat on the closed toilet seat, his elbows on his knees and his hands steepled over his mouth. He stared dead ahead. Ten perched on the edge of the bathtub, both legs bouncing. She bit her thumbnail and stared at her watch.

"One more minute, Keller."

"You look. I don't want to look."

"We're both looking. Thirty seconds. Get ready."

"I can't, Harper. I'm freaking out over here."

"You're freaking out? I'm freaking out. Okay it's time. Come sit over here."

She patted the space next to her. When he sat, she reached for the narrow white stick on the counter, her eyes averted.

"Close your eyes, Keller."

"They're closed."

"Count of three, we open them. Whatever it is—"

"Whatever it is, we'll be fine."

"One. Two… Three."

They opened their eyes, looked at the little rectangle window and saw…

"Oh, my God. We're going to have a baby, Harper."

"I'm going to be a mom." Ten's eyes shone as she faced Nick. "You're going to be a dad."

"Holy shit. Let's go tell your pop."

They opened the door to find Charlie, Kablooey, and Margot, their faces beaming and their tone only slightly apologetic.

"We're having a baby," exclaimed Charlie as he clapped Nick on the back hard enough to propel him forward.

"Okay, well, technically *we're* having a baby," said Nick, rolling his shoulders and wincing.

Ten whacked his arm. "Technically, *I'm* have a baby, and you all get the easy part."

Margot hugged her. "I know I'm not the real grandma, but I'm so excited to spoil this little peanut. In fact, I think I'm going shopping right now. Charlie, let's go."

"Ah, gee, Go-Go, the Parkinson's is acting—"

"No, it's not. You took your medication and you just said you feel great. Now let's go."

"Congrats, you two. Uncle Kablooey is gonna baby proof the whole place. When I get done, ain't nobody gonna get hurt on anything. I gotta get to the hardware store. See you two later."

Nick tried to get a word in, but the trio was in full manic mode. Tenley raised one palm to her forehead and the other on Nick's shoulder.

"Don't bother, Keller. Just let them go."

Shouts and door slams echoed through the house. When it was quiet again, Ten and Nick faced each other.

Ten said, "We're having a baby."

"You, me and baby make three," sang Nick.

"And Charlie, and Margot, and Kablooey…"

"And Fitz, and Lizzy, and Ludo…"

"Okay, okay," said Ten. "You, me, baby, and a whole lot of others. Oh, my God, I've got to call Tomi Lynn, and Lee and—"

"Go on, go on. I promised to help Max at the bar for a while anyhow. See you soon, wife."

They kissed. "See you soon, husband. And don't tell Max before I tell Lee we'll have that playmate for Rider after all."

Nick left Tenley to her phone calls. Once he left, she stood before the full-length mirror, turning this way and that. Placing her hand over her still flat belly, she spoke.

"Hi, there, little alien. It's your mama. Listen, kid. This isn't going to be the most conventional life, but I promise, it'll be filled with so much love."

EPILOGUE PART TWO THE WEDDING

They planned the nuptials for sunset. The early morning rain shower came and went. At Ten's insistence, Max and Lee were separated overnight—she at Ten's for a girl's night in, he at home and playing poker into the wee hours with Nick, Charlie, and Kablooey.

Lee stood on Ten's lanai, gazing out over the ocean. The sun had risen heavy and slow, and the beach—raked clean and smooth at dawn—welcomed the handful of runners and strollers. Lee smiled, peaceful and content with coffee mug between her hands and paradise laid out before her.

She inhaled the salty air until her lungs were full, then released the breath through her lips.

"Nervous?"

Ten closed the French door behind her and joined Lee.

"No. Is that weird? Shouldn't I feel nervous?"

"Not when you're certain. You and Max are perfect together. There's nothing more *right* than you two."

"Besides you and Nick, you mean."

"Ah, Keller and I are yin and yang. We'll always push and pull each other around. It's our kind of perfect, but it's different than yours."

"We both found the persons we're meant to be with," agreed Lee.

They sipped their coffee in silence. A minute later Margot and Lucy came out singing Chapel of Love at the top of their lungs, mimosas in hands.

"One for you. And one for you, girlies." Margot handed them each a glass. "Raise em up. To Lee on her wedding day. May you and Max have a beautiful and blessed life together always."

"Here, here," said Lucy.

"Cheers to one hundred years," said Tenley.

She raised her glass but didn't take a sip. Her eagle-eyed friends took notice.

"What was that," said Lucy.

Lee studied her with squinted eyes. "Wait, did you drink last night? Ladies, I don't recall seeing Ten drink last night, either."

Margot smirked behind her glass and she did a little dance, unable to contain herself any longer. She squealed, "Tell them before I burst, Ten."

Lee and Lucy gasped.

"Oh, my God, you're pregnant," said Lucy.

Lee clapped and jumped up and down. "You're giving Rider his playmate!"

Ten accepted the flurry of teary hugs with good humor. "Oh, God. You all are going to be the crazy aunties, aren't you?"

"Yep. Mad-hatter with a purse and credit cards crazy," agreed Margot.

They spent the day in spa heaven, thanks to Margot's connections—manicures, pedicures, and massages—interrupted only by the phone calls from Nick, saying he forgot his tie. Then Charlie, who wanted Margot to order food for them. Last from Max, who just wanted to tell his bride he loved her.

"Promise me, kid, you two will always be this damn romantic," said Margot.

"Yeah, you two make me feel like there's hope still for me," said Lucy.

"Aw, sweetie, of course there is," said Ten.

Lee frowned. "But what about you and Carlos?"

They all looked at her. Lucy was the first to laugh, then the rest joined in.

"Oh, honey," gasped Ten in between gails, "how could you not know Carlos is gay?"

"Very, very gay," laughed Margot and Lucy.

Lee opened and closed her mouth, then slapped her forehead. "That makes so much more sense now."

After the laughter died down, a sly look came across Ten's face. Her eyebrows twitched in Margot's direction and Margot gave a subtle nod.

To Lucy, she said, "Sounds like you've been seeing a lot of Josh lately. What about him?"

"Josh? What—no, no, no. He's adorable. And sweet. And so hot, but... no. And I've only seen him a lot because he's been coming in for smoothies, like, every day."

"Mhm," said Tenley, "and you realize they have a smoothie bar at the gym? You know, *the gym he works at?*"

"Yeah but—he said—no. I just have more to offer than the gym."

"You said it, sista," said Margot.

Ten and Margot high-fived.

"Stop it, that's not what I meant. Anyhow, it's too weird. Like, I don't know, breaking girl code to date someone a friend has dated."

"Oh, puh-lease. Do you actually need my permission? You know I'm married and with child now, right? Okay, listen. You may date Josh if you want to. There."

Lucy tried to hold back a smile and failed. Then, to Lee, she said, "Me and Carlos? Really? Girl, I can't even."

When a knock on the door came, they all shouted, "Come in," and Jacqui peeped her head in.

"Hi, I'm here to do the bride's hair?"

Lee motioned her in, introducing her to everyone. Only Ten knew that Lee wanted to fix her ex-husband up with the gorgeous hair stylist, and when Jacqui turned her back, Ten gave an emphatic thumbs up.

In whispers, she filled Margot and Lucy in on the plan. From that point on, the women were excessively friendly and nice to Jacqui. After the fourth offer to get her a cocktail or make her a plate, she called them out.

"Okay, ladies. Either you're all a little tipsy, or something is up. Lee, does this have anything to do with Kenny?"

"What? I—who?"

"Kenny. The guy you were married to for, like, twenty years or something. He's going to be here tonight, isn't he?"

Lee mumbled, "Fifteen," and shrugged her shoulder. The other women became deeply interested in the flowers on the table. Jacqui sighed.

"You're all crazy, you know."

"Not the first time someone has told us that, strangely enough," said Margot over her shoulder.

Jacqui picked up the curling iron and said, "How do you know I'm not seeing anyone?"

Lee met her eyes. "Are you?"

Jacqui looked away. "No, but—"

"Perfect. Neither is Kenny. Plus, he's been moping since his friend Fuchsia went to perform on some cabaret cruise thing."

"I'm not dressed for a wedding, Lee."

"You look perfect. It's casual dress."

"You're not going to let me back out of this, are you?"

Lee thrust her chin out and said, "Nope. Not a chance."

Thirty minutes later Lee's hair fell in loose beach waves with dainty periwinkles braided into a halo around the crown. The women gasped and fawned, and Jacqui stepped back with a look of satisfaction as she inspected her work. A couple spritzes of hair spray, and Lee was officially ready to say I do.

"Knock, knock. You kids decent?"

"Come on in, Charlie. We're ready," called Margot.

"Aw, just look at you, kid. You know, my own daughter denied me the joy of walking her down the aisle, but at least my Tenley Too is giving me the honor."

Ten rolled her eyes. "Oh, Daddy, don't be such a baby. I'm giving you a grandchild. Doesn't that make up for eloping?"

Charlie sniffed at her and said, "I suppose. Now, if I got to pick the little tikes name, that would—"

"Forget about it, old man. We're not naming my child Hurricane. At least, not for the first name." She winked.

"Fair enough. Now let's go get this girl married."

Led by the others, Charlie and Lee came down the stairs arm in arm. She suspected she looked like an elf beside the giant man and quite liked it. At the garland draped gate leading to the beach, they paused. The music began.

Charlie tipped his head down and said, "It's not too late to change your mind, kid."

From behind them, Tenley swatted his arm. "*Daddy.*"

"What? Every girl about to walk down the aisle should have a dad telling them they can change their mind."

Lee giggled. "It's okay, Ten. Thank you, Char— Dad. I am one hundred percent certain that Max is the man I want to marry."

Charlie winked. "Then let's get you married, sweetheart."

The ceremony was short and sweet, held before those they loved. Just as the sun set, they exchanged vows.

"Tenley Grace, I promise that from this day forward, I will cherish and love you with all my heart. Our life will be full of music and laughter, crazy friends and happy children, big dogs and little dogs, and pretty much anything your heart desires. I love you, Lee."

"Maxwell Thomas, I promise, from this day forward, to never, ever give you a dull moment. I promise to love you and take care of you and be your best friend for life. And I will cherish every precious moment of our music and crazy friends, happy children and dogs filled life together. I love you, Max."

Carlos, their officiant, said, "By the newly vested powers in me by the State of Florida, I pronounce you husband and wife. Kiss your bride, handsome."

Laughter and applause erupted as Max and Lee kissed for the first time as a married couple. Rose petals fluttered through the air as they walked up the aisle. Lee stopped and took a quick scan of the group.

"Okay, ladies. Get ready."

On the count of three, she tossed her bouquet over her shoulder. Whoop and shouts, then a chorus of '*aww*' s followed. Lee spun to see a mortified but grinning Jacqui holding the flowers. Lee may or may not have aimed intentionally. She'd never tell.

The reception followed at the Harper's. With Rider held between them, Max and Lee's took the floor for their first dance. Nick, who served as best man, and Tenley, the matron of honor made toasts.

"To our sweet, wonderful Max, who more than anyone I know, deserves all the happiness in the world. And to our Tenley Too. Our connection is unusual—"

Someone shouted, "You can say that again."

When the laughs died down, she continued, "—and could've turned out very differently. But whatever strange twist of fate brought us here, I'm so glad it did. You're one of us, now. God help you. We love you both."

Ten raised her glass. "To Mr. and Mrs. Rivers!"

Cheers rose into the night once again and the music began. Lee spied Kenny and Jacqui talking in a corner and smiled with a self-satisfied glee.

"Mrs. Rivers, are you playing matchmaker for your ex-husband?"

Max's eye twinkled with merriment as he contemplated his wife.

"I am, Mr. Rivers. Is that weird?"

"Incredibly. But also, sweet. They look good together. Nice job, wife."

"Thank you, husband."

Nick and Ten joined them. A moment later the photographer appeared, camera poised and clicking.

"How about a picture with just the two Tenleys?"

Max and Nick stepped aside, and Lee and Ten posed. When he moved on to capture candid shots, the women laughed.

"We will forever be called that, you know," said Lee.

Ten said, "Kind of sounds like the name of a book, doesn't it?"

Lee studied her friend a moment. Something in the arch of her brow, the mischievous grin caught her. A flash of memory—Ten typing at lightning speed on her laptop the day Lee told her she was pregnant—dropped her jaw.

"You're writing our story, aren't you?"

Ten shrugged, then nodded, now suddenly bashful. "Is that all right? I mean, you don't mind, do you?"

Without hesitation, Lee said, "Write it, Ten. The whole thing. I can't wait to read it."

Ten breathed a sigh of relieve. "Good. I finished it last night. Nick's publisher wants to see it, but I wanted to ask you first."

Lee teased, "You wrote three hundred pages, *then* asked?"

"Three-hundred-twelve, to be exact. I figured you'd be okay with it."

Lee hugged her friend. She suspected this wouldn't be the last of surprises from name-twin. Not that she minded. The brain tumor that meant to kill her had taught her how to *live*. Having her story told would've horrified the old Lee, but the new Lee embraced it.

***

For a time, Ten questioned the *why* it all. Providence or coincidence? The more she wrote, the more she realized a simple truth. It didn't matter. Whatever it was—the universe or chance—so many lives were changed for the better by one mistake. Neither Ten nor Lee sued the doctor whose error send them on this wild ride. In fact, Lee sent him an invitation to the wedding, which he declined. With a gift.

Ten's relationship with her mother did not grow without hitches and bumps but grow it did. Tomi Lyn was there for the birth of twins Rose and Grace, and for the official book launch of Tenley Times Two. They are in the works of co-authoring a book about Tomi Lyn's life.

As for Charlie the Hurricane Harper, he finally married Margot. They've never been happier. Charlie's Parkinson's remains under control thanks to advances in treatment. However, he often gives his wife credit for keeping him healthy, happy and active. They're terribly sweet to see… and sometimes a little nauseating.

Kablooey reunited with his on-time flame, Diana 'The Diva' Valentine at Charlie and Margot's wedding, and the sparks flew once again. They now own a second gym together where they teach wrestling to under-privileged kids.

Josh is the gym manager of Kablooey and Diana's gym. He dated Lucy for several months, until they both agreed they made better friends than lovers. He's still looking for a steady girl.

Carlos found his calling and is the most sought-after wedding officiant in the county. He finally went out on that date with Diego and they are now a couple.

Kenny and Jacqui began dating the night of Lee and Max's wedding. They're engaged and plan on marrying after their fourteen-day cruise—a gift from their dear friend and star of The Divine Ones, A Tribute Show on Majestic of the Seas, Fuchsia Featherbottom—or maybe *on* the cruise, depending on how much they drink.

Not long after Ten gave birth to Grace and Rose, Lee and Max had another child, a girl they named Harper Chance. Those three girls grew up together—under the weary and protective eye of big brother Rider—to cause a great deal of trouble. But that's another story...

THE TWO TENLEYS

ABOUT THE AUTHOR

Elsa Kurt is the author of more than a dozen novels, including her beloved Welcome to Chance series. When not writing, Elsa mentors new and aspiring authors through her Path to Authorship program. If you are a new/aspiring author, visit Elsa at elsakurt.com or email her at authorelsakurt@gmail.com. If you've enjoyed this book, please consider leaving a review on Amazon, Goodreads, or BookBub!

ARE YOU IN A BOOK CLUB?

Elsa loves her book club readers, so if your book club is reading any of her books, reach out to Elsa at authorelsakurt@gmail.com for a free signed copy for the hostess & to set up a live video chat with your group.